HEAVEN'S EMBRACE

HER ANGELS BOOK 1

ERIN BEDFORD

J. A. CIPRIANO

WANT TO GET THIS FREE?

<u>Sign up here.</u> If you do, I'll send you some free short stories.

Visit Mika on Facebook or on the web at MikaDaniels.com or visit Erin on Facebook or on the web at ErinBedford.com.

ALSO BY ERIN BEDFORD

<u>The Underground</u>

Chasing Rabbits

Chasing Cats

Chasing Princes

Chasing Shadows

Chasing Hearts

<u>Fairy Tale Bad Boys</u>

Hunter

Pirate

Thief

Mirror

Stepbrother

<u>The Celestial War Chronicles</u>

Song of Blood and Fire

Visions of War and Water

<u>The Mary Wiles Chronicles</u>

Marked By Hell

Bound By Hell

Deceived By Hell

Tempted By Hell

<u>The Crimson Fold</u>

Until Midnight

Vampire CEO

Granting Her Wish

ALSO BY J.A. CIPRIANO

<u>Starcrossed Dragons</u>

Riding Lightning

Grinding Frost

Swallowing Fire

Pounding Earth

<u>The Goddess Harem</u>

The Tiger's Offer

The Wolf's Hunt

The Dragon's War

<u>Justice Squad</u>

Miracle's Touch

<u>Her Angels</u>

Heaven's Embrace

Heaven's A Beach

Heaven's Most Wanted

The Shaman Queen's Harem

Ghosts and Grudges

1

1
____

Heavenly Arms brought in the normal kind of crowd for a Thursday night, and I mean normal if you think drinking before five P.M. just so you could get a chance to find out if your boyfriend was cheating on you was normal. That was the kind of crowd that was always there for me.

I tried my best to focus on the blonde woman in front of me. Samantha something was three shots deep and bawling her eyes out about which guy she should choose, the rock star or the billionaire. Cue eye roll. I wanted to be sympathetic, I really did, but the tingling trailing up the back of my thighs in a teasing manner took all my give-a-fucks from my mind.

Shoving at the hand, I tried to play it off as scratching an itch, but that only earned me a dark chuckle in response. Of course, the woman in front of me had no idea what was going on. Samantha something couldn't see the gorgeous hunk of a man currently playing bartender behind me. No one could. Besides, me that is.

How'd I get so lucky?

"Quit it," I hissed under my breath, hoping not to attract attention to him. Not that anyone could see him, they would think I was just talking to myself. Again.

"Make me," a husky voice laughed, the same warm tingling from before brushing the back of my neck and sending a shiver down my spine. Lucifer, fallen angel, and Devil extraordinaire loved to come to work with me, and sometimes, he meant that literally. Why he thought torturing me was more fun than the very deserving victims of the underworld, I'd never know. Not that I could complain because Lucifer was some serious man candy. Too bad he wasn't corporeal enough to back up his deliciousness. Talk about clit tease.

"What was that?" Samantha something slurred, her brow creasing.

"Nothing," I replied with a strained smile as I

tightened the hair tie around my dark locks. I imagined it was Lucifer's cock and his eyes were begging me for mercy. The Devil at my beck and call was a pretty dream indeed. "You were saying something about your boyfriend?"

"Oh, yeah." Samantha sniffed before breaking into a scowl. "So, the rock star, Damien, he's got the whole bad boy thing going for him, but there are all the groupies to contend with. Who wants random women pawing at their man? Not me I tell you!" As she slammed her glass down on the counter, I winced.

Please, don't break the glassware.

Samantha ignored my silent plea and continued on her tirade, "Then there's the billionaire, Eric. He's so hot you could crack an egg on him and watch it sizzle! But" - she pointed a finger at me with a pop of her lips - "he works all the time. Sure, that means more money, and that's good and all, but I need attention! So, here I am pouring my heart out to a damn psychic bartender! No offense," she added at the last second before drinking deeply from her glass, her manicured nails tapping an annoying beat on the bar top.

"None taken," I said between clenched teeth. She wasn't the first to use my services and then talk shit about them, and she wouldn't be the last. Although, I wouldn't have any extra services had it not been for the devil on my shoulder, so to speak.

I'd always been special … or cursed. Depends on how you look at it. It wasn't like I saw random things that weren't there. I see one specific kind of thing. Angels to be exact. I've tried to ignore them, but once they realize you can see them, they don't give up.

Like Lucifer.

As if knowing I was thinking of him, the fingers on the back of my thighs dipped beneath my skirt and brushed the line of my soaked panties. It wasn't much more than a sensation, a barest of caresses that never really gave more than a taste of what it could feel like to have Lucifer really touch me. I'd gone years with these angels following me around, teasing me with touches but never able to give me more. To say my body was a bit on overload would be an understatement.

As Lucifer's fingers got awfully close to my center, I sucked in a breath and closed my eyes briefly. Don't moan. Don't moan.

"Are you okay?"

My eyes snapped open and landed on Samantha's worried face. I could just imagine what I looked like, standing there behind the bar with a glass I'd washed about a dozen times in my hand with an expression of desperate ecstasy. It would make anyone think I was crazy … which they did, often.

"I'm great." My voice went up an octave as Lucifer's thick fingers brushed my bare, sensitive skin. Clamping my legs closed, I mustered up a grin. "Just need to use the little ladies' room."

"Oh, okay," Samantha drew out as I ducked out from behind the bar, my three-inch heels clacking loudly on the wood floor. I shot a glare at the dark-haired devil following on my heels with smug satisfaction on his lips.

Did I mention that fallen angels count as angels to me? My powers didn't discriminate or make much sense, for that matter. They really should have come with an owner's manual, or at least a warning label.

Warning: Psychic powers will attract delicious angelic man meat with a horny meter of over nine thousand. Massive quantities of panties required!

Thursday nights were slower than most, but I still had to push my way through a crowd to get to the bathroom. I nodded toward Bret the door hop, a large fellow with a soft spot for musicals and appletinis. He was an odd fellow, but I could always count on him when some drunk idiot got out of hand. Too bad he couldn't help me with my need for a little stroke and poke. Bret liked a big dick more than I did.

The bathroom door closed behind me, and I could finally get the smell of body odor and dried beer out of my nose. Honestly, the bathroom wasn't much better. Really, Heavenly Arms was less of a hole in the wall and more crowded dive bar with an extra order of stink.

A woman was standing at the sink washing her hands as I barged in. I paused for a moment, surprised anyone else was in there. I shook it off, giving her an awkward little greeting before darting into the stall. The stall wasn't big enough for one person, let alone me and the Devil, who thought he was so slick popping in there as I shut the door.

"Get out of here," I hissed, pointing at the stall door. "I actually do have to pee, you know." And maybe rub one out, but he didn't need to know that.

"Well, then by all means." Lucifer crossed his arms over his meticulous designer suit and leaned back against the door. Where the Devil found clothing like that was a mystery. Maybe Devils Do Prada?

Wherever those clothes came from, they knew exactly how to wrap his tall frame and broad shoulders into a nice package. Not that he didn't already have a nice package. He had been pretty prompt at informing me of that fact when I'd dared to insult his size.

My traitorous mind flashed a reminder of what exactly lay beneath those pants and my face heated. Lucifer's smile grew, and I held a hand up so he couldn't come closer.

"I'm not going to go pee in front of you." This time I said it a bit louder than I meant to. Outside the stall, a loud scoff sounded, followed by the banging of the bathroom door.

"I don't think you really need to go," Lucifer taunted.

We stared at each other for a moment, each one of us trying to make the other yield. After a few seconds, my eye started to twitch. Damn Devil and his overpowering stare.

"Fine, you win."

"I always do." Lucifer smirked.

With a frustrated sigh, I pushed through Lucifer,

causing a full body tingle as we merged for a moment, and then made my way out of the stall.

"Don't you have some poor souls to damn to hell or something?" I ducked down to see if someone was in the other stall before heading to the door. Clicking the main door's lock into place, I spun around only to find Lucifer inches from me. How'd he get so close so quickly?

"Oh, bathroom sex, this will be fun," Lucifer commented with a chuckle, earning himself a glare from me. "I don't damn souls, you know that. Humans damn themselves, I simply punish the wicked." He smirked, caging me against the door. "All kinds of wicked. I know for a fact you have been a very naughty girl." Lucifer licked his lips, his eyes making a cursory path down my body. My skin heated from where his gaze roamed, sending lightning pulses to my clit.

Tired of being permanently turned on with no relief, I scowled up at him. Lucifer had more than a foot on my height, and even with my heels, my eyes only reached his collarbone which made trying to be intimidating a bit tricky.

"Instead of being a cosmic-sized tease, why don't you do your job and give me a break?" I crossed my arms over my chest, trying to put some distance between the two of us.

"Where's the fun in that?" his voice lowered, and his dreamy brown eyes flicked down before meeting mine once more. More than any of the others, Lucifer had always been harder to keep my sex drive under control around, probably because he was, you know, evil. Or supposed to be. So far, he just liked to drive me into a lust-crazed haze while I served beer to the undeserving populous. Damn sadist.

"Job security, of course." My voice came out more breathless than I had intended, and I cleared my throat, my shoulders rolling back. "I pretend to be this all-powerful psychic while you get to get your rocks off fucking with unsuspecting humans. That was the deal, remember? Or are you tired of playing with us already?"

His grin broadened, and if I hadn't already soaked my panties, he'd have just destroyed them. Then he turned it up a notch as he leaned in close. "I'll never be tired of playing with you." His mouth skimmed mine as he spoke, the buzzing sensation not even close to enough friction to tide me over.

I was dangerously close to saying fuck it and let him watch me, anything to relieve some of the tension in my clit. There had to be a first time for everything, right?

As luck would have it, before I could inch my finger into my panties, the door banged loudly behind me. Jerking away from him, I clicked the lock and opened the door to see a long line of pissed-off women waiting.

Face flushing, I coughed nervously. "Uh sorry, shy bladder." I moved past the angry mob and back toward the bar which had become way more crowded since I'd left. My co-bartender, Terry, a self-proclaimed cowboy who refused to wear anything but boots to work, shot daggers my way.

Mouthing an apology, I jumped back behind the bar and began to help him with the sudden rush. I was thankful for it because it kept my mind off my raging libido. Not that it would help with the Devil looking deliciously tempting just inches away. Not being able to touch the angels didn't mean they couldn't torture me in their own way.

Ignoring someone talking in your ear every five seconds was hard. Especially when you weren't trying to look like the crazy person most people thought you were.

They made plenty of situations awkward for me. Not for them, though, because they didn't give a crap. They're both non-corporeal and invisible which meant they could do whatever the fuck they wanted, and I just had to deal with it.

Still, having them around had their upsides… usually.

"So, a house rum and coke? Coming right up," I said, moving to grab a glass and as my fingers closed around it, Lucifer's hand touched my waist, startling me. The glass slipped from my hand and shattered on the floor behind the bar, and as I stared at it, I nearly blew a gasket. That was the third fucking glass tonight.

Not caring who was watching, I spun on my heel and growled, "Do you mind?" I pointed at the glass. "This is your fault."

Chuckling in his devilishly handsome way, Lucifer backed off a few feet and sat down on the stool in the corner I'd specifically set out for him. "Sorry, love. I just can't help myself." He waggled his dark eyebrows. "Can't blame a Devil for trying."

Rolling my eyes, I turned back to the waiting crowd only to be greeted with curious stares. Mouth gaping, I tried to find the words to explain, but good ol' Terry was there in a split second to save the day.

"Don't mind Jane, ya'll. Being psychic makes

her seem like a hog out of its pen sometimes." Like usual, Terry's Southern accent made the customers settle, and as they started returning to their shots and conversations, he clapped his hand on my shoulder and flashed a lopsided grin at the still curious. "Price of being gifted."

"More like cursed," I muttered under my breath before giving the crowd a small smile. Then I tapped my temple with one finger. "Don't worry, folks. My hog is back in its barn. You can go back to drinking your life away."

Terry clapped his hand on my shoulder again, a bit harder this time in warning before going back to his side of the bar. I didn't really know if Terry believed I was psychic or not, but he played it up for the crowd like we all did. My so-called psychic abilities brought in people who wouldn't otherwise be caught dead in the place. Often people with more money than sense, which also meant more money for all of us. So, Terry, like most of the others had made a capitalistic decision. Play up the charade.

"Sorry about that," I said, sliding the newly made rum and coke across the bar to the guy who had ordered it just before my little mishap. He was in his mid-thirties, buzzed head, and had his eyes too focused on the other man in front of him to pay attention to me or the drink he'd ordered. He also wasn't fooling anyone into thinking he was just there for a good time. He had cop written all over him.

"Have you seen this girl?" The cop playing undercover, badly I might add, held a picture up to one of our regulars. Dan, I wanted to say his name was, but it could have been Fred for all I knew. Good with names, I'm not.

"No way." Dan/Fred shook his head before swigging from his beer bottle. His eyes were glazed over but deliberately not looking at the cop.

I didn't have to turn around to know Lucifer was behind me again. I could feel his presence warm against my back causing a not so unpleasant feeling of pleasure to ripple down my spine.

"He's lying," the Devil whispered into my ear, his voice a soft coo that tickled all my senses and made me want to lean back into him. That alone would have made it take me a second to realize what he'd said, but honestly, it was really his fingers dancing down the side of my body, tempting, teasing.

"Are you sure?" I said, using the words to give me time to pull away and collect my thoughts.

Honestly, I needn't have asked. The king of lies always knew.

"Yes," he said, appearing on the bar between us, pointing down at the guy though no one else could see or hear him. He could be dancing the cha-cha on the bar in nothing but a tutu, and no one would bat an eye. "It's written all over his sallow face."

"Okay." I set down the glass I'd just filled in front of its owner and moved toward the cop. Even in heels, the bar top barely reached below my chest. If I didn't wear them, the girls bounced off the bar all day, and trust me, that was not a pretty picture.

"Hey, Dan." I batted my eyelashes at him, but the moment he saw me, he choked on the beer he was drinking, and his face paled. Yeah, I get that reaction a lot.

"Hey, J-Jane." He coughed and cleared his throat, his eyes becoming skittish. "What's up?"

I guess I did get his name right. Go me!

Giving him my best, no-nonsense look, I placed my elbow on the bar top before propping my chin on it. "You know what's up, Dan. Or do you want me to tell this nice police officer?" I grinned and slid a sly look at the cop who looked startled by my presence.

Dan shook his head rapidly. "No, no. It's all

right. I got this." He turned back to the rightly confused officer and said, "I saw her, but that's it. She left with some tall, balding guy just after happy hour last Friday."

Stunned by the guy's admission or maybe by my looks - hey it could happen - the police officer stood from his stool and hooked his belt with his thumbs. Why did all cops do that? Did their pants not fit right?

After a small adjustment, he gestured for Dan to stand up. "I think we need to take a ride downtown. You can give us a better description of the guy you saw."

Dan begrudgingly stood and shot me the stink eye.

Can't please everyone.

The police officer didn't leave right away. Instead, he turned back to me with a suspicious glare. "I don't know what you did to make him talk, but thanks."

I gave him a two-finger salute and a grin. "No problem. All in a day's work."

He snorted but didn't say anything more as he turned and followed Dan out of the bar. Shrugging, I didn't let his reaction bother me. Most people didn't get me or my sense of humor. Or my psychic powers. Which, by the way, are fake. Like, pay-by-the-minute fake. The only abilities I had were seeing sexy angels who really needed to get laid — oh wait that's just me. Though, I wouldn't complain if they were the ones doing the laying.

Sadly, though, they're the ones with all the powers, I just monopolize on them for my own gain.

Fair trade in my opinion and that's the only one that counts. Right?

So, yes. That's why I put up with them. For the best cause, really. Me. And you know, for the spank bank.

2

"Hey, Jane, you have a second?' Terry asked, shuffling uncomfortably as he finished locking the door.

"What's up?" I asked, shoving my share of the tips into my pocket.

"I was wondering." He paused and scratched behind his ear, his usual tell when he was nervous. He sighed, as if talking to me was a big effort. "Now, I'm a good Christian fella, so don't go tellin' my mama I asked you this, but is all your psychic stuff for real?" He glanced up at me as if I might shine a light on his otherwise meager existence. "The way you know if them folks is lyin' or not. It's really sum'thin'."

I forced back the sigh that threatened to come

out. I hated when people I knew and liked asked me this. The last time I'd told someone the truth about my abilities, I'd needed to change jobs. And I liked my job. Sure, being a bartender wasn't anything special, but it was better than stripping. Which I could totally pull off. Seriously, I could. Check out my butt! Totally bounce-able.

But the point was telling people about my angelic admirers was never a good idea because no matter what I said, I wouldn't really change Terry's perspective on the world, *and* he would never look at me the same way again.

"No, Terry," I said finally. "It's not real. I'm just really perceptive." My answer had the desired effect.

Terry's shoulders uncurled, and he stood a bit taller like he knew it all along. "That's what I thought." He scoffed before turning back toward his car. "Well, carry on, Jane. I won't keep you."

I watched him for a moment, half tempted to call him back and tell him I was lying, but I didn't. I knew what it was like to have your world so shaken up that you thought you were going mad, and I wouldn't wish that on anyone.

"What are you are looking at?" a smooth voice from my left said, making me jump in place.

I spun and glared at the brown-haired Adonis who had just appeared out of nowhere. The angel Gabriel gave an apologetic shrug. Out of all the angels I could see, Gabriel was the least full of himself, which was the only reason I didn't get on to him for scaring the living daylights out of me. If it had been Lucifer, he'd have done it on purpose.

I shook my head and muttered, "Nothing."

Pulling my keys out of my purse, I headed for my car, a five-year-old blue Kia. Sure, the battery needed to be jumped multiple times every winter, but it got great gas mileage… and it was paid off, so bonus?

Sliding into the driver's seat, I didn't bother waiting for the large angel to slide into the other seat before I started it up. I fiddled with the radio, though after two A.M. there wasn't anything good to listen to.

"You should really put your seat belt on." Gabriel's chastising tone made me grin. I couldn't be mad at Gabriel no matter how annoying he might be. Gabriel was like a surfer dude and a big brother all rolled into one. Though, I'd never seen him as a brother, because one doesn't think of their brother's abs as lickable. Not to mention he, like

Lucifer, had more horniness in him than the entire student body at the local high school.

"You're an angel. Aren't you supposed to guard me against danger?" I shot him a grin and instantly regretted it. Lucifer's teasing from earlier came back with a vengeance and looking at Gabriel's chestnut colored locks hanging over pale green eyes only made matters worse. Damn, when God created the angels, he only used the good bits.

"Doesn't work that way, doll." Gabriel chuckled and draped an arm over the back of my seat, giving me a nice tingle as a result. "Telling you to put your seatbelt on is about as much as I can do as far as divine intervention."

I snorted at that. "And trying to get into my pants isn't?"

"That's just fun." A sinful grin covered Gabriel's lips. A smile like that shouldn't look so good on an angel of God.

"So, I'm just fun to you guys now?" I scoffed and shook my head. "Never mind Jane, who's slowly going insane from permanent horniness. We're just having a bit of fun. No big deal."

"Aw, come on now, Jane, don't be that way." Gabriel tried to tap me under the chin, but all it did was set my teeth a-buzzing. I jerked away, keeping my eyes on the road. "We don't do it to torture you."

I snorted.

"Okay, so maybe Lucifer does, but he's the Devil. What do you expect?" Gabriel shrugged from the corner of my eye, and I got an eyeful of his muscular chest straining beneath his t-shirt. Out of all the angels, he wore the most casual clothing. Jeans and t-shirts were his go to. Occasionally, he'd throw a plaid button up over it, but that was rare.

"So, if you aren't here to torture me, why are you here?" I asked as I pulled into the parking lot of my apartment complex. A bartender's salary didn't cover much, even with the extra tips from my psychic readings, but I'd been lucky in finding this particular apartment. The area wasn't horrible, and while the manager was lazy, he didn't charge me more than my meager studio apartment was worth.

Gabriel shifted toward me, drawing my attention to his remarkable eyes once more. "Can't I just want to enjoy your company?"

I leaned in as well, a hint of a smile on my face, causing him to smile as well. When his breath brushed mine, I said, "No." I pulled away and got out of the car without waiting for him to follow.

Sadly, cheap rent came with downsides. Parking

sucked most days of the week, and while safer, the apartment was located on the third floor. After a long day of serving drinks, those steps were killer on my short legs, but seriously, my butt has never looked better!

As I fumbled with my keys to unlock the door, Gabriel leaned against the wall beside me. I didn't even bother to wonder how he had gotten up here so fast as I continued our conversation from the car.

"I just feel like you guys could be doing something else with your eternal lives, you know?" I unlocked the door and pushed it open before stepping into the apartment. "I mean, if I were an angel, I wouldn't be hanging around with the likes of me. I'd be out scouting the hottest men. Seeing all the best shows. Maybe even go to a nude beach." I paused, tapping my chin. "Actually, definitely going to a nude beach. Or the changing room at Thunder Down Under." I waved a hand. "You know, something like that."

I threw my bag on the two-person breakfast table. It banged against the backside of my beat-up couch, barely keeping from spilling over. While my apartment was full of hand-me-downs and thrift store specials, I had saved up to buy a few nice things. Like my television. My thirty-two-inch T.V.

equipped with surround sound made me feel like I was living in Middle Earth during my *Lord of the Rings* marathons.

There were a few things I cared for: emergent entertainment and good water pressure. Since one of those things couldn't be helped, I did what I could about the other.

Unfortunately, my apartment didn't allow for a fancy bed, or I'd have my dream four-poster equipped with a princess style canopy. Instead, I was stuck with a twin bed shoved between the wall and entertainment center/nightstand. Even if I could let one of the celestial beings enamored with me show me the hotter side of Heaven, it'd be a bit awkward since the bed barely fit me.

Gabriel laughed, startling me. All thoughts of getting one of the angels to fit into my bed flying from my mind.

He shook his head as he chuckled, making his hair fall over his eyes.

"Been there, done that. Not much fun when no one can see you." I rolled my eyes as I kicked my heels off, losing a few inches. Gabriel's fingers curled over my shoulders, and he leaned down until his breath brushed hot on my neck. "Or feel you."

"I can't really feel you either, you know." I

cursed myself for sounding as turned on as I felt. Months of these guys hanging around me had made me drawn as tight as a nun's habit, with no chance of trying to relieve it. You try masturbating when you know angels could pop in on you at any second. Not fun.

"You can feel me more than any other human." One of Gabriel's hands slid down from my shoulder to wrap around my waist, sending a buzzing down my spine and into my naughty bits. I could see the hard line of his cock, and I forced back a groan. Did they all have to be so perfect?

Trying to get my mind off the temptation presented in front of me, I moved out of Gabriel's embrace and went to the fridge. I needed something cold to bring down this heat.

"Don't you have other angels? Females that could help you out in that department?" Even as I made the suggestion, part of me growled. The thought of some gorgeous female angel touching my guys pulled out the jealousy in me. Who's attached? Not me.

I dug around in the fridge until I found my left-over Chinese and a bottle of five-dollar wine. Not even bothering to get a glass, I unscrewed the top of the wine and took a big swig. I tossed the Chinese into the microwave as I pretended Gabriel wasn't watching me like a starving animal.

"Female angels are stuck-up bitches too absorbed in the Almighty to pay the rest of us any mind," Gabriel practically growled as he stalked toward me. "You aren't anything like them." He grinned. "You're so much better."

I snorted. "So, I've been told." Inside, I was dancing at Gabriel's praise. Take that angel bitches.

"Come now, Jane." Gabriel brushed against my body, as close as he could get without being inside of me. Which honestly wouldn't be a bad thing. "Don't you want to explore what could be between us?"

"Believe me, what I want to do to you guys has less to do with exploring and more to do with exchanging body fluids." I smirked.

"We could make that happen." Gabriel's hot gaze burned along my skin, making me squirm.

I turned my head away from him to take another large drink from my wine bottle. I had a nice little buzz going now, which did nothing to dampen the party in my pants. "Unless you have some way of becoming solid that I don't know about, I think you're just blowing steam out your ass."

"You think an angel would lie?"

"Of course not. Well, maybe Lucifer." I smiled. "In any case, shouldn't you be spending your time, you know, up there and not with me?" I tried to remind him of the big boss man in the sky. Wouldn't He be pissed if his angels loved someone else?

Gabriel shrugged. "We have a duty, but it's not the same thing." When my baffled expression didn't change, he sighed and rubbed a hand over his face. "You're not immortal, you wouldn't understand."

"I could if you'd explain it to me." I tried to coax him, but he wouldn't budge.

"Humans don't really get the whole indebted for your entire existence thing," Gabriel explained. The way he lumped me in with all the other humans irritated me like I was just like everyone else.

"Well, excuse me for being human," I clipped. Wouldn't understand, my ass. I could see freaking angels. How could I not understand?

Taking my wine bottle with me, I stomped into the bathroom and slammed the door shut. It wouldn't keep the angel out, so I didn't bother locking it. Still, I hoped I had done enough to make him leave me alone, at least for tonight.

When he didn't immediately follow me inside, I knew he'd gone. Well, that was fine… I needed to calm down anyway, and I knew just the thing. I turned on the shower.

Sure, I'd have to reheat my food, but I'd rather have soggy Chinese than spend another minute in my soaked panties.

I dared to take my time showering for the first time in months. I had PTSD from Lucifer popping in unexpectedly, making every shower into a tits, pits, and ass ordeal. My hair had split ends from not being properly conditioned.

"Why have you upset Gabriel?"

I screamed and clutched my arms to my chest. Shoving myself as far into the corner of the shower as possible, I glared over my shoulder at the blond angel.

"What the fuck, Michael?" I snapped, getting even more pissed off by his bored expression.

Crossing his arms over his chest, he leveled a serious, considering look at me that made me shift in place. "My apologies, I didn't realize you were bathing. Gabriel came home quite distraught, and you know how much I dislike hearing him whine. Alas, here I am." He gave an elegant shrug.

Dressed in tight-fitting jeans and a black V-neck,

Michael could give any Sexist Man Alive a run for their money. Of course, he'd actually have to be alive for that, but you get the picture.

"I can't have this conversation right now while my junk's hanging out." I glanced at him once more and frowned. "How are your clothes not getting wet right now?"

Michael huffed as if my question was more exasperating than it actually was. "I'm not corporeal, but ..." He reached out and slid a finger along my slick skin and then rubbed his thumb against that finger. He held his hand up for me to see the wetness there. "I can feel what has already touched you."

I gaped at him. "Huh?"

"Don't try to think too much about it. You'll give yourself a headache." Michael shoved his hands in his pockets with a frown. "Not saying your dumb… it's just too complicated to bother trying to understand."

"Fair enough." I threw the shower curtain open and grabbed a towel. Quickly drying off, I grabbed the discarded pajamas from last night off the floor. Not even bothering to put on underwear, I pulled on the shorts with little bananas on it and a tank top with the words 'Spank the Monkey' written across the chest in yellow. They'd been a gift from my best friend Mandy before she became a party pooper by getting a real job.

Man, I missed her.

Though quiet, I didn't miss the heavy gaze on my body as I marched back out of the bathroom. Like I'd thought, Gabriel had gone home, wherever that was, but sadly he'd left his guard dog behind.

When it first got out that I could see them, Gabriel showed up at my house as eager as a pup, but when we found we couldn't touch each other, he'd scurried away with his tail between his legs. Of course, not long after, Michael had showed up all glowery and domineering, demanding, like now, to know what I'd done to Gabriel.

"I didn't do anything to Gabriel," I said, repeating the words I'd had to say far too many times lately. I grabbed my Chinese from the microwave, not even bothered that it was lukewarm now. Plopping down on the couch, I slurped noodles, making sure to be extra annoying with each slurp.

Michael didn't even seem bothered as he stood in the middle of my apartment. "I don't know why you bother to fight it."

"Fight what?" I asked through a mouthful of

food. Maybe if I disgusted him enough, they'd get the message.

"Destiny, of course." He smiled at me, and I swear my heart stuttered.

"I'm hardly fighting anything. Believe me, if ya'll could touch me, really touch me, we would be having a whole different conversation right now." Actually, I hoped we wouldn't be talking, that our mouths would be preoccupied with other things. Not letting on to what I was thinking, I added, "Also, I don't believe in destiny." I avoided his eyes as I dug into my Chinese, the bottom of the container coming faster than I'd hoped.

"Jane, there's a reason you can see us. Feel us." His voice warmed, and I dared glance up for a moment. Michael's gaze caused my whole body to warm as his voice caressed my skin. "We are drawn to you. I don't know why, but I've known for a while not to fight what the Creator has planned for us."

I snorted, standing up. "Well, destiny can kiss my ass, all implications implied. I choose my path, no one else." I paused and raised a brow. "Unless you're here to show me exactly what destiny can do?"

Ignoring my innuendo, Michael said, "You can hide behind your free will all you like, it won't change the truth." With Michael as close as he was, even his incorporeal self made my nipples harden, just from his presence.

I'd had just about enough of my body's reactions for the night. I needed a break. Trying to get as much space between us as possible, I made for the kitchen. Tossing my sadly empty Chinese container in the trash, I scooped up what was left of my wine.

"Don't try to pretend you don't crave us like we crave you," Michael commanded, prowling toward me. "Our senses are far superior to a mere human's. I can smell your desire from here."

"Who's pretending?" I countered.

"We both know we could do more… things that don't involve touching." Michael's gaze raked over me as he spoke, making all sorts of bad ideas dance through my mind.

"That sounds like it might make things worse and not better," I said, swallowing hard as my eyes traces the hard lines of his body.

"Perhaps." I didn't think it was possible for someone to sound sexy and haughty all at the same time, but Michael had, you know, right before he vanished completely.

"Figures," I grumbled at the empty spot he left.

Unscrewing the wine bottle that had seen more action than me in one night than I had in the last year, I chugged it until it was gone.

Crawling into bed, I smirked as I remembered my conversation with Michael, but this memory had a decidedly different outcome, one that I'd love to let happen. Hell, it was one I *wanted* to have happen.

3

Thankfully, the rest of my night was quiet, and I meant that in a completely no-angels-in-my-house kind of way. I didn't even notice I'd fallen asleep until the sun beamed in through the curtains, blinding me through my eyelids. I cracked them open enough to grab the blanket and yank it over my head. That small amount of time was all I needed to catch a glimpse of a blurry figure sitting on my raggedy old couch. Freaking wonderful.

"If you're a robber, get on with it," I grumbled from beneath the covers. "There's nothing here to take unless you like cold Chinese and a pathetic attempt at a half decent life."

"Now, I wouldn't say that, love." The sinfully

delicious sound of Lucifer's voice wafted through the fibers of the blanket. "I would say you have a more than decent life. You have me after all."

Snorting, I sat up with the blanket clutched to my chest. "You would think that, but any sane person would have committed themselves by now."

I should be used Lucifer's gorgeousness. I should not get girly tingles every time I see him in his devilish splendor. The way he sat on my couch, both arms draped over the sides, one leg crossed over the other as if he owned the damn thing, made my traitorous thighs press together.

Lucifer's dark eyes glinted with amusement, and for the first time, I noticed how his nostrils flared as if checking the air. Irritation filled me as Michael's words resurfaced. Fucking angels and their enhanced senses.

Note to self. Buy obnoxious perfume to cover up the scent.

Not bothering to berate him for his omission of said abilities, he's the Devil so he wouldn't admit it anyways, I stared him down. "What do you want?" The exhaustion in my voice came out as a growl.

Standing from the couch, he towered over me as he took the few strides to my bed. Without warning, he sat down next to me, causing the mattress to dip considerably. I clutched the blanket to me even tighter, cursing myself for not putting on proper underwear last night.

"I want what all men want," Lucifer murmured, his eyes darkening as they promised horribly naughty things I'd no doubt enjoy but regret when they were over.

"A big breakfast?" I countered, trying to get rid of the stifling tension in the room. "Do you guys even eat, like real food? For that matter, do you even follow human laws? If not, what's the point of following social niceties or even wearing clothes for that matter?" My rambling was cut short when I had somehow come full circle to the point at hand.

"If that is what you wish, I can accommodate such a request." His lips curled into a wicked grin as he reached for the buttons of his white dress shirt.

I reached out and grabbed his hand before he could disrobe or at least tried to. It ended up going through his chest. I couldn't help but wiggle it around a bit. I blame the wine from last night. Too much wine and not enough water. I was dehydrated, I couldn't be held accountable for my actions or run-away mouth.

"Please, keep your clothes on, my heart can't take much more of your endless teasing." I pressed my mouth into a thin line and patted at him awkwardly, promptly killing the mood. "I don't have time for you today in any case."

Lucifer, never the one to be disheartened, leaned forward, and purred, "Really? I could make time if you'd like."

Pretending his tone didn't make my core gush like Old Faithful, I cocked my head to the side. "You can do that? Stop time, I mean? Because really that would make my day a whole lot easier. You have no idea how many things I have to get done, and there is hardly any time before I have to be at work tonight."

Seeing he didn't get the desired effect, Lucifer sighed, the first signs of agitation causing lines on his face. "You really are something else, Jane."

"So, I've been told."

"I'm serious. Here I am, pouring my heart out to you ..." I snorted, causing him to glare in my direction.

"And you make jokes," Lucifer sneered. "You've admitted you want me, and I know that if I could touch you right now, you'd fall to pieces, and yet you defy me. Why?"

I shrugged with a wry grin. "It's either that or go insane. A girl can only take so much foreplay without a promise of a climax before she goes crazy. You might be into the pain game, but I'm not a masochist. Now about the time thing …"

Exasperation covered his face as he ran a hand through his dark hair, tousling it even more than before. "No, I cannot literally stop time for you to get more errands done. The paperwork alone for such a feat wouldn't even make up for what you could provide me with in return."

Pouting at his proclamation, I pushed my covers back and crawled down the bed to get off. "You know you really shouldn't make empty promises. Getting a girl's hopes up and everything. Here I thought you were trying to woo me." I shook my head in mock disgust.

Lucifer didn't answer but watched me with cursory eyes. I tried not to let it bother me as I dug through the never-ending pile of laundry laying on the floor. I picked a shirt up and gave it a testing sniff, satisfied with its lack of B.O. I tucked it and a pair of jeans underneath my arm, before grabbing a pair of underwear from a different pile, not so barbaric as to wear dirty panties. With my clothes bundled in my arms, I headed for the bathroom.

I sat the bundle on the toilet and found my discarded bra from last night. Peeking out of the bathroom door, I searched for my unwanted shadow. When I found his spot on my bed empty, my shoulders eased, and I pulled at my tank top. Before I got it over my breasts, a sneaking suspicion made me pause.

Spinning around, I placed my hands on my hips and glared at a smirking Devil sitting on the bathtub lip.

"What does a girl have to do to get some privacy here? Do I need to get a priest in here, because I will," I warned. I wouldn't really, I didn't think it would work for one, and two, I'd miss him if he was gone.

"You act as if my being here is a burden." The fallen angel palmed the rim of the tub, leaning back as he stretched his legs out. My bathroom wasn't big enough for his large frame and me to coexist without touching so his pant legs brushed mine.

"No, the fact is that if I were a guy, I'd have a raging hard-on twenty-four seven, and sometimes a girl needs a little privacy." I sighed and hugged my clothes to my chest tighter, feeling vulnerable from the intensity of his gaze.

"If you wanted privacy, all you had to do was ask." The teasing in his voice made me want to scream.

"Lucifer, stop torturing Jane." Michael's voice made me frown. Michael looked the exact way he had last night except without the dangerous undertone he'd left on. The look on his face was a mixture of annoyance and pity. Both emotions irritated me. I was the one who should be annoyed. They were the ones popping into my life and making my life and my panties hell, not the other way around.

"I apologize for Lucifer's behavior. He does not know when enough is enough." Michael's apology made me realize that Lucifer had decided to leave. It happened so suddenly, that it actually took me a minute to realize he'd left.

I turned back to Michael watching as he leaned against the door frame while I pulled out my toothbrush.

"No shit. He's the Devil," I said sarcastically as I poured toothpaste onto the brush and shoved it into my mouth. "You know, you guys really need to get a life. 'Cause I only have one and I can't spend every second of it beating off horny angels." With my mouth full of toothpaste, I wasn't sure how much of it Michael actually understood, but he answered anyway.

"I understand your displeasure," he said with a

raised brow as if he weren't sure he got my emotional state correct, "but might I offer a bit of advice?"

I spat, gave him an impatient look in the mirror, and shoved the toothbrush back in my mouth.

"While you're no doubt feeling overwhelmed …" When I made a rude noise, Michael's eyes narrowed. "There is a reason we were brought together. Whether to simply satisfy our deeper urges or for some more divine purpose, I do not know, but it might help you relax a bit if you …" His brows furrowed. "How is it you humans say? Flick the bean? I'd be happy to provide visual stimulus."

I sputtered at him and leaned to down to spit once more, but by the time I stood again, he was gone. Wiping my mouth on the towel, I pulled on my clothes like my life depended on it before stomping out of the bathroom. Of all the insufferable ball sacks. Did he not think I had already thought of that? I wouldn't be wound so tight otherwise.

This wasn't the first time I'd encountered angels, but none of them wanted to do me then, let alone paid much attention to me at all. I was a kid, for crying out loud. But when I told my parents about it, they just laughed it off. It wasn't until much later that my mother let me know that she too saw angels. Guess it runs in the family.

Bet she didn't have to worry about horny angels though.

Snatching my keys and purse off the counter, I slammed the door behind me. I almost fell to my knees and cried with happiness when I turned to find a blonde bombshell waiting for me with two coffees in her hands. With greedy fingers, I took the offered cup and took a big drink, not bothered that it burned my tongue as the caramel chocolate mixture hit my taste buds.

"Bad night?" the blonde said with a smile. Amanda or Mandy for short, my best friend in the entire universe and maybe even the entire multi-verse, if one believed in such things. Which I didn't, or I didn't think so.

Where I was short and scrappy, she was built like an Amazon with golden locks and a badge that allowed her to shoot people for real. Like without repercussions. I really needed to get me one of those.

"You have no idea," I moaned as I held my coffee cup in both hands like it was the answer to all my prayers. "How did you know I needed this?" I glanced her way with suspicion in my voice.

Mandy's quizzical look confused me. "It's Friday. You always need coffee on Fridays."

The reminder of the day destroyed all pleasure of the caffeinated orgasm happening in my mouth. Mandy was right. She always was. It was Friday, which meant it was time for a visit with my parents.

Don't get me wrong, I loved my parents, but they could be a little much.

Swallowing down another gulp, I hoped it would quench the anxious feeling in my stomach, but it only made it worse. This morning's fight with the angels only added to the damper on my day.

When I told Lucifer that I had things to do today, I hadn't been lying. I'd be expected at work by four, but before then, I had to get groceries and buy more underwear, something I sadly found myself doing more and more of recently. But before any of that, I had to go check in with the good old fam.

"But why are you here?" I asked, making my way down the three flights of stairs. "You rarely have time to meet me for drinks, let alone do emotional handholding now that you're a hotshot detective."

When we stopped in front of my car, I turned and waited for her explanation. Mandy stood next to me with her blonde hair pulled back tight in a bun, her legs encased in too nice of pants for a visit and, dear God, a blouse, yes, a blouse. I didn't know how I didn't see it before.

"You're here for work, aren't you?" I accused. I glanced down at my cooling coffee with utter disdain before giving her the evil eye. "This is bribery coffee, isn't it?"

"Jane," she started, but I didn't want to hear it.

"No, no." I shoved the coffee back into her hands cutting her off. "Take your dirty coffee and go. I have places to be for, as you reminded me, it's Friday." I clamored into the car and tried to slam the door, but she caught it with her lightning-fast reflexes. I blamed the police training. They had to replace parts of their trainees with robots to do what they did every day.

"Listen, Jane, just give me five minutes," Mandy pleaded with me.

I pursed my lips. "Two."

"It's your fault really," Mandy started, and I already didn't like where it was going. "Clemons was down at the Heavenly Arms working over this guy who was clamming up tighter than you did that one time at Jimmy Mitchell's kegger, you remember that?"

"Thirty seconds, Mandy," I warned, tugging on the door.

Her eyes widened, and panic seeped into her voice as her words quickened. "And he said some five foot nothing bartender helped him. That's when he started asking around and found out you're a psychic, which I told him was ridiculous because you'd have told me if you were ..." She trailed off as I stared at her. Letting go of the door, she sighed. "Why are you telling people you're psychic, Jane? You can't even tell when someone's bluffing at poker, let alone be a lie detector as people are claiming."

I just kept staring at her, hoping she'd come to the right conclusion on her own. I really didn't want to have this conversation with her in the middle of my apartment parking lot. Besides, she should know me better than that.

Like I knew she would, Mandy finally figured it out and stomped her foot like a petulant child. "Oh, come on Jane. I thought you were past all this. Weren't you taking pills or something?" Now, her eyes had real worry in them.

Waving a hand to the passenger side, I waited until she climbed into the car before shutting my own door and cranking the car. "It's not something you really get past, Mandy."

"But you stopped talking about it, so I just assumed you were better." Mandy crossed her arms over her chest, her ample bosom straining against the buttons of her blouse. I forced back a grimace at the very thought of the word. I should burn her shirt on principle.

As I eased down the road, I explained, "Just because someone stops talking about something doesn't mean it's gone. You didn't want to know, so ..." I fluttered a hand in the air.

"And the pills?"

My fingers tightened on the steering wheel. "They make my head feel funny like I'm numb from the inside out."

"But they helped, didn't they?" There was a kind of hopefulness in her voice that I hated to destroy.

I shook my head sadly. "No, Amanda. They didn't."

4

My parents lived in a gated community, the kind that had a guard at the front who always looked at me like I was up to something. Of course, that was probably because I regularly egged his station when I was younger.

I was a bad kid. So, sue me.

The lawns were perfectly manicured with elaborately shaped bushes, like bears and other animals. When I was little, I had a reoccurring nightmare where the bushes were alive and were chasing me with pruning shears, screaming, "Just a little bit off the top!" Sometimes I still woke up in hot sweats shouting, "Cut 'em at the roots." One of those times Lucifer had been there. Wasn't that some-thing fun to explain?

In my honest opinion, the only bush shaping should be your own and only to keep it neat. None of that landing strip crap or fancy shapes. I once knew someone who did a lightning bolt. Like Harry Potter was going to come ravage her vagina. Some people.

Unfortunately, those kinds of people were the kind who lived in my parent's neighborhood. It wasn't mine. It'd never been mine. I'd always been the odd one out. Parents didn't want their kids playing with the weird kid, go figure.

"Jane."

Mandy's voice startled me out of my thoughts, and I met her concerned gaze. "What?"

"Are you going to go in or stare at it all day?" She unbuckled her seat belt and opened the car door, not waiting for me to answer before she got out.

We'd arrived at my parent's house already. I hadn't even noticed. That's how much I disliked being here. I laid my head against the cool rubber of the steering wheel, contemplating skipping today, but a knock on my window stopped that thought. Grumbling to myself, I unsnapped my own seatbelt and climbed out of the car.

The two-story house before us had an off-white color to it just like the majority of the other houses on the street. I knew one thing. If my parents ever did kick the bucket and left me their house, I was painting it neon green. I'm a rebel that way.

"I don't know why you came," I said, walking up the little stone path my mom had made me spend a whole week of summer vacation putting in.

"For moral support, of course." Mandy kept up with me easily, her long legs making my speed walking seem like a languid stroll.

"I thought you were here on police business," I reminded her with a look of disdain.

"Well, that too, but that doesn't mean I can't be here for you now that I'm already here. Besides, I love your mother too. I'd love to see her." The sincerity in her voice was the only thing keeping me from snapping her head off.

Mandy wasn't only my best friend, but she was my oldest friend. We've been attached at the hip since fourth grade when booger-eating Jeffery Polts broke up with her in front of everyone. He'd called her a giraffe neck and a wet kisser. Why they were kissing in the first place, I chalked up to bad parenting and rated R movies. But while everyone laughed at her, I had an epiphany.

See, I'd always been the smallest. The last to be picked at games and the one who everyone tried to bully. That was until they realized I wasn't some weakling who'd just take it. I'd never laid back and taken anything in my life. Ask my dentist; he's got the bite marks to prove it.

Jeffery Polts had been right about one thing. Mandy had a giraffe neck and legs. She was too large for our grade, and that worked for me just fine. So, I walked straight up to Polts and punched him in the nuts. Safe to say that no one laughed at Mandy after that and we had been best friends ever since.

"She'd want to see you too," I murmured as we stopped at the front door. I'd always loved our door, one of the few things I did care about in the house. With a large wooden frame and slender windows on either side, it was the perfect place to spy on the neighbors. Of course, my mother didn't even bother hiding, she'd sit out on the yard in a lawn chair, binoculars in hand.

Yeah, my mom was that kind. I rang the doorbell, a sound I could hear even from the doorstep. Like a foghorn, that thing was. I always joked that it was partly why my father was hard of hearing. Also, it sucked when you were trying to sleep in on Saturdays and your parents were social butterflies. It'd wake you from a dead sleep.

We didn't have to wait long for the door to open and reveal my father, Richard Mehr. Greying on the sides, his hair was still holding strong even pushing sixty. He wore glasses that he was constantly pushing back up the bridge of his nose. Luckily, I had perfect vision. I didn't think I'd rock glasses like Richard Mehr did.

"Janey!" My dad cried out, opening the door all the way to let us in.

"Hey, dad," I smiled up at him despite myself. I barely stepped into the house before I was pulled into a warm hug. I let him hold me for a moment, taking in the scent of him. Modeling glue and peppermints. "Been playing with airplanes today, have we?" I asked as I pulled back.

The guilty grin on my dad's face made me grin too. "I'm a surgeon, I have to keep my hands in tip-top shape."

"Sure, that's the reason," I joked.

"Hey, Mr. Mehr," Mandy stepped in behind me, my dad closing the door behind us. "How's it going?"

"Good, good. Hospital keeps me busy. I might not get to perform surgery as much anymore but being the head of the surgical department still keeps me on my toes." My dad might complain about his work, but I know he loved it. He'd never be happy doing anything else but helping people. Maybe a pilot. Or a plane designer. They had those, right?

"Well, come on in." Dad ushered us into the house. "Want something to drink?"

"Sure," Mandy and I both said, looking at each other and grinning.

"I've got some iced tea. The housekeeper, Beatrice, made this morning."

"Tea!" Mandy and I both rushed to say, this time bursting out laughing.

My dad chuckled and shook his head. "It's like you two are teenagers all over again." When we reached the kitchen, he pulled down some glasses and poured us each some. "Not that I'd wish for you two hellions to be running around here all the time, but it is good to have some younger people in the house again."

My expression softened as I smiled at my father. I really should visit more often, but with my father's busy schedule and my evening shifts, it was hard to find an appropriate time to come. Maybe if I ended up consulting for the police, then I'd have more control over my schedule. Visiting more would be nice.

Handing both of Mandy and me our iced teas, my dad pushed his glasses up the bridge of his nose. "Now, make sure you go see your mother. She's in the solar."

"As usual," I muttered, earning me a warning look from dad.

"Now, Jane. You be nice to your mother. She doesn't need any of your sass."

I held my hands up in defense. "When have I ever sassed?"

My dad pursed his lips. "Only every other word that comes out of your mouth."

He had me there. "I don't have any reason to sass mom. As long as she doesn't start talking about grandchildren, we'll be peachy keen."

Dad snorted. "Good luck with that. I'll be in my office if you need me." Left to our own devices, Mandy and I stood at the breakfast bar drinking our tea.

"So, you were here on police business, right? Something to do with that officer at my bar last night?"

Mandy glanced at me as if she just remembered that was the whole point of her visit in the first place.

"Oh yeah. Right. About that." She cleared her throat and put her arms behind her back. Something I suspected she learned from the police academy to keep her from fidgeting. "So, that pompous idiot Clemons went to the police station spouting off about you and how you had gotten that guy to spill the beans ..."

"Dan."

"Yeah, him." She nodded and then finished her iced tea. "Anyway, he went on about how he'd been working on Dan for a good hour, and all it took was a sentence from you, and he was more than happy to spill his guts." Mandy laughed. "He'd have told us his social security number if asked."

Putting Mandy and mine's glasses in the sink, I rolled my eyes. "I doubt that very much."

She shot me a chastising look as we headed out of the kitchen. "Anyway, the captain made inquiries about you and your little psychic act. He thinks you check out and now ..." Mandy groaned as if it really hurt her to say the next words. "Now, he wants you to come on to help with the case."

We passed through the living room which was

filled with seats that made your butt feel like it had died and gone to Heaven. But even the best cushion could become hard as a rock if you sat on it long enough. I should know, I'd done a lot of sitting here in my day.

"What case?" I asked, the solar finally coming into view. I could just make out my mother's dark hair sitting by the window. She always did like the outdoors.

"That's classified until you accept the job."

"Job? You mean with pay and everything?" I lit up like a birthday candle at the prospect of money.

Mandy pressed her lips together tightly, saying in a clipped voice, "Yes, you would be on the Blessed Falls Police Department payroll as their resident psychic."

"I'll do it." I didn't need to know what all the job entailed, it had to pay better than bartending, though I'd still do that in the evenings. I'd have to talk to the boss about shortening my hours though; that wouldn't go over well.

Mandy grabbed my arm, stopping us before we could get to my mother. "There's a problem with that."

"What? I'd have to get stripped searched?" I

cocked a brow at her and grinned. "Because I'd be up for that if the guy were right."

Shaking her head, I could tell she was trying not to smile, but she finally sobered. "Stop trying to make me laugh. I'm serious, Jane. You see things that aren't there. That doesn't make you psychic."

"How do you know? You don't know the extent of my powers. I could have laser vision and see straight through your pants there." I put my fingers on either side of my forehead and stared hard at her. "I can see that you are wearing your Wednesday underwear on a Friday." I clicked my tongue with a shake of my head. "Naughty naughty. You should do your laundry."

Mandy shoved my hands down from my head with an impatient sound. "Jane, be serious. You can get in a lot of trouble pretending to be something you're not, and how would you help anyway? Have your angels go find her?"

"Actually, for your information, the guys each have special abilities that they lend me for such occasions." I opened my mouth to keep going but snapped it shut.

"What is it?" Mandy asked.

I growled and shoved a hand through my hair.

"We're kind of on the outs right now. Probably have to fix that."

Mandy snort laughed. "You're on the outs with your imaginary friends? How is that possible?"

Shooting her a sideways look, I clipped, "They were getting handsy, which is incredibly frustrating when they're not only super hot, but can't actually touch you." Not waiting for an answer, I started toward my mother once more.

I sat next to her on the bench. She didn't look away from the window even as the cushion dipped my way. I placed a hand on her shoulder, startling her. Her grey-blue eyes focused in on me and a smile spread across her lips, showing the lines on her face.

"Jane, dear. When did you get here?"

"I just got here." I hugged her slightly before sitting back on the bench. "Mandy's here too."

"Hey, Mrs. Mehr." Mandy sat on the chair opposite of us. "It's good to see you."

Penny Mehr was a beautiful woman. People say I am the spitting image of her, but she's better. Even at her age, she was still the most devastatingly beautiful person I'd ever met. But she's my mom, so I might be biased.

"Mandy, you've gotten so tall." My mom smiled at her. "And you've made detective I see."

Mandy shrugged and scratched her ear, her tell that she was uncomfortable with my mom's compliments. "Yeah, just recently actually."

"I'm going to help them with a case," I blurted out suddenly. Mandy gave me a warning look, but I ignored her. "Some guy at the bar liked how I got his suspect to talk, and now they want me to use my special powers to help them solve cases."

"One." Mandy held her finger up. "One case. And you haven't even been accepted yet."

"Working for the police, oh that sounds exciting." My mom said as we pretended like we hadn't even heard Mandy. "Are the boys all right helping you? I assume you did ask them?"

"Uh …"

"They're fighting," Mandy interjected, and I glared at her. She smiled smugly, her arms over her chest.

"Fighting?" My mom glanced at Mandy and me. "Jane, what did you do now?"

I scoffed. "Why does it have to be something I did?"

My mom leveled a look at me.

"Fine." I threw my hands up. "I lost my temper

and blew up on them. But you would have too if they kept flaunting their hotness at you but never put out."

Most mothers would have chastised me for being crude but not my mother. She threw her head back and laughed, a tinkling sound that warmed my heart. "Oh, to be young again. I remember when Raphael used to hang around me all the time. I was half in love with the angel by the time your father came around. But let me tell you," - she fanned herself with a wistful smile - "he was hot."

"Mom!" I wrinkled my nose. "Gross."

"So, you can talk about your sex life, but I can't?" My mother rolled her eyes. "How *is* your sex life going? Outside of the boys?"

I did mention my mother sees angels too, didn't I? Great isn't it? Not really. While it was nice to have someone else with the same ability that I did, when mom got all nostalgic it could get awkward fast because you know… moms.

"Non-existent, mom." I hoped that would be the end of it, but of course, it wasn't.

"You know, if you need help finding someone, the Petersons' son is back from the Middle East and I'm sure would be happy to see you." She had a twinkle in her eyes that made me think she had more than seeing in mind for him and me.

"Darrell?" I asked, a disgusted look on my face. "He used to throw mud in my hair."

"He was ten," my mother reminded me.

Crossing my arms over my chest, I scowled. "Doesn't matter."

We sat and talked for a bit longer, my mom interjecting different guys I could date at every chance. See why I needed coffee this morning? She made me feel like a broodmare. Would it be so bad to let me decide when I wanted to have kids? Maybe I wouldn't have them at all. Wouldn't tell her that though. She'd disown me. Well, she was too nice for that. She'd give me a hard look. Probably.

As Mandy and I made our way back to the car, she asked, "Why don't you stop paying attention to the angels? Your mom seems to have moved on from them. Why can't you?"

I shrugged. "I gave up fighting what I saw a long time ago. They're there. No use trying to pretend they aren't." I heaved in a large breath and let it out. All the tension from seeing my mother dissipated. At least something good came from all that therapy. Grinning like an idiot, I glanced at

Mandy and started the car. "Are you hungry? I'm starving."

Mandy let out a puff of air and chuckled. "Of course, you are, you bottomless pit."

"Hey, don't hate me because you're jealous of my fast metabolism." I held up a hand in her direction.

Snorting, Mandy whipped out her phone and started scrolling through it. "You say that when you're in your thirties and have a muffin top and cavities. Can you drop me back off at your apartment? I left my car there."

"Sure, and what about the case?"

She lifted her head from her phone and sighed. "I can't seem to stop you when you have your mind set on something plus the captain wants to meet you, so I don't really have a choice in the matter."

"Damn straight."

Mandy glared at me. "Anyway, can you come by the office before work?"

Brows furrowed, I thought about it. I still needed to buy groceries, I had nothing in the apartment. I'd eaten the rest of what I had last night which in the grand spectrum of things probably wasn't the best anyway. Who knew how long that Chinese had been in there for?

I also needed to reconcile with the guys. I'd been a right bitch to them this morning and last night. They wouldn't be happy to lend me their services so I could make money unless I apologized. Sure, they were endless flirts, and I had blue ovaries because of them, but really it wasn't their fault they couldn't touch me.

"Jane?" Mandy snapped her fingers in front of my face.

Blinking, I nodded. "Yeah, I can do that. I've got a few more things to do, but I'll come by before I head to the bar."

"With your ... companions?" I almost smiled at how hard it was for her to admit that they existed.

My lips tipped up in what I hoped was a smile. "You leave that to me."

5

———

There was only one place I wanted to go after dropping Mandy off, and coincidentally, it happened to be the same place I knew the guys would show up.

The Tasty Orange.

It not only had the best frozen yogurt in town but twenty-four different flavors with even more options for toppings. I'd made the mistake of one time getting one of everything in the same bowl. I was drunk and spent the following few hours in front of the toilet.

Since then, I made sure to stick to the basic flavors, but I still visited the Tasty Orange more often than my own family. There was just something so soothing about the white and screaming orange walls, the vinyl seats, and the smell of sugar in the air. It catered to all types of people. The young, the old, the hung-over. The Tasty Orange could turn anyone's day right side up, which I needed after another of my mom's talks about guys and grandkids.

Luckily for a Friday, it wasn't filled to the brim with people. A couple sat in a corner, their eyes firmly on their phones while their bowls of froyo melted before them. I didn't need to be a psychic to know they weren't going to last. They were almost as sad as the cashier who looked like she'd had just about enough of our crap. As long as she only had gummy bears as a weapon, I wasn't too worried. The family of four might cause me some issues though. Toddlers didn't know when to pretend something wasn't wrong, unlike adults, who were fluent in denial.

I sat at my table eyes down as I tried to inhale as much sugary goodness as possible before I had to give up my dignity. I had no doubt the guys would make this as painful as possible for me. They might be angels, but that didn't mean they weren't devils at times.

"You humans and your sweets," Michael said as

he appeared. He made a face across from me and shook his head.

Gabriel appeared next, his leg pressed against mine, sending a tingle down my thigh. "Leave her alone, Michael. Just because you can't eat doesn't mean you should judge others."

"Yeah, lighten up, Mike." Lucifer became visible, taking the seat next to Michael, much to the angel's displeasure. "If Jane wants to kill herself with sugar, that is her business."

I took a sugar covered bite just to spite him, making an over exaggerated moan as it filled my mouth. It had the desired effect. All three of them tensed beside me, leveling me with heated stares. But it wasn't just them staring at me, the family of four looked at me like I had gone off my rocker.

Removing the spoon from my mouth with a pop, I shoved it into the bowl and dug around in my bag. I pulled out my phone and earbuds, putting one bud into my ear.

"What's that for?" Gabriel asked next to me, his head cocked to the side like a curious little boy.

I kept my eyes on my food as I muttered, "So, I don't look like a freaking psycho talking to myself."

"What's wrong?" Gabriel asked, his brows

furrowed. Of course, he'd be the first one to notice my mood.

Slouching further into my seat, I frowned at my dessert as if it had been the one to upset me. "Just not a good day."

All three of them became intensely interested in my face, and I tried not to be offended. While they could easily go to the top of my most hated list, the guys, even Lucifer, were way too caring for me to stay mad at them. Besides, I was supposed to be there to ask them a favor, not talk about my problems.

Of course, I couldn't just jump right into it. I had my dignity, at least some of the time, and an abnormally large amount of candies in my bowl.

"I've been wondering something," I started, glancing up from my bowl, their intense stares making me shift uncomfortably. "If Lucifer is the Devil, should you two really be talking to him?"

A mixture of confusion and surprise greeted me. Lucifer slumped back into his seat, and somehow, he made even that look good. Fucking angels.

"That's what you called us here for?" Lucifer pouted, his arms crossed over his chest.

Ignoring Lucifer's whining, Michael, as usual, took the lead. "Lucifer may be fallen, but he's still our brother. We are not forbidden from interacting with him nor would we want to do so."

"Why not?" I quirked a brow. "He's the Devil. Bringer of evil. Torturer of damned souls. Isn't that completely against everything you and Gabriel stand for?"

"You're forgetting dangerously sexy and a generous lover." Lucifer slid his hand down the front of him, a lewd grin on his lips as he looked me over. Well, there went today's panties.

Gabriel chuckled, ignoring Lucifer's display. "You watch too many movies. Lucy isn't any more evil than the rest of us. He just doesn't know how to stay out of trouble so God, our Father, assigned him to monitor Hell. He doesn't even get to torture anyone." Gabriel's laughter caused Lucifer's jawline to tighten and grind his teeth. Sour subject for him apparently.

"What did you call us here for?" Lucifer growled, clearly trying not to lash out at Gabriel.

"Chill out, Lucy." Gabriel threw an arm over the back of my seat, a lopsided grin on his face. Where his arm touched me warmed and buzzed. I leaned back into the feel of it. Who needed a masseuse when you had your own personal angel to use? I did mean in a happy ending kind of way.

"Don't call me that," Lucifer snapped, pulling me out of my pleasure-filled delirium.

"He's right, Lucifer. Jane called us here for a reason, and we can at least give her the courtesy of explaining herself in her own time." Michael tapped his fingernails on the table. How no one else heard him was beyond me. How they could touch anything at all didn't make much sense. One of those things I shouldn't think too much about.

I squirmed in my seat, the attention and my train of thought not helping me relax, but I might as well get it over with. Off like a band-aid as they say.

"I wanted to apologize." Jeez, those words were hard to get out. "I realize I came down really hard on you guys, and it wasn't fair to blame my raging libido on you. It's not like you get me all hot and bothered on purpose ..." I trailed off before shoving another spoonful into my mouth to give myself a moment, the grins on their faces making me squirm. "Anyway," I said through a mouthful of froyo, "I kind of need your help."

"Ah, here it is," Lucifer smirked, unbuttoning his suit button to lean forward on the table. "So, what is it you need? Not making enough money at the bar anymore? Want to strike out on your own?"

The laughter in his voice made me sink further into my seat. At this rate, I'd be on the floor before I even finished eating.

"Oh, don't pout." Gabriel grinned and leaned in close. "We're happy to help. I always thought the bar was too loud anyway. You should find a nice little shop where you can sell those little bobbles, you know, good luck charms and such. Humans like that stuff, right?"

I giggled and waved him away. "No, it's nothing like that. My friend, Mandy, works for the police department, and they wanted my help finding some girl."

Lucifer's eyes lit up, his grin turning wicked. "Oh, this is about that bloke from last night, isn't it?"

I nodded and, shoving my hair away from my face, sighed. "Look, you don't have to help me if you don't want to, but I thought you guys might want to do something else besides hanging around, you know, up there." My eyes shot to Lucifer who raised his brows. "Or in your case, down."

"We'd be glad to help you, Jane," Michael said in a way I didn't like.

"I feel a 'but' coming on." I held onto my bowl until the cold burned my hands.

Michael smiled. "Of course, there will be certain conditions for our assistance."

I couldn't hold back my groan. "What do you want?"

"A kiss." Lucifer jumped in before Michael could answer. "Each. At a time and place of our choosing."

"I can get behind that." Gabriel grinned broadly.

My lips pressed together tightly, the very thought of kissing any of them made my blood run hotter than it should with so much frozen yogurt in my system. Believe me, if kissing them had been a real option, I'd been in a four-way lip lock already, but sadly the only lip action I was getting was with my wine bottle. Why they were putting it on the table now, I wasn't sure. Maybe something to look forward to if they became corporeal?

Or Lucifer just wanted a new way to torture me.

"Fine, but" - I held my finger up before they could speak - "how the heck do you expect to do that when you can't touch me?"

"Let us worry about that." Lucifer grinned like a maniac.

"Works for me," Gabriel said, disappearing without another word.

"Agreed." Michael inclined his head before disappearing as well.

"Hey, wait a second," I called after them, but they were gone leaving me alone with Lucifer. My gaze snapped to his gloating face. "And then there was one. Are you going to give me some answers?"

Lucifer grinned until I could see his molars, making me wiggle in my seat. "All I will say is that I look forward to working with you and collecting my payment." He licked his lips, and I would be lying if I didn't say that it turned me on. A part of me really hoped they could find a way to touch me, that part of me was also jumping up and down like a cheerleader on prom night.

"Freaking angels," I muttered, and as if my day couldn't get any worse, my phone rang. I found the cord of my earbuds and the very not-plugged-in end of it. Not even taking the chance to look at the audience I probably had earned myself, I picked up the phone. "What's up, Mandy?"

"Hey, Jane. Are you coming by soon? The captain could really use your ... expertise." I could hear her exasperation even through the phone.

"Sure. I was about to head that way now. Just

gathering my ..." I glanced at Lucifer who didn't seem in any hurry to get moving. "... spiritual energy."

Mandy snorted. "Yeah, all right. See you soon."

Putting the phone away, I didn't bother saying anything to Lucifer as I got out of the booth. I threw my melted goodness away, sadness filling my stomach at how such a delicious thing had gone to waste. I hated adulting.

I made my way to the parking garage of the mall the Tasty Orange resided in, not caring if the Devil was following me or not. I'd need one of them at the police station, but I was pretty sure they'd show up when I called. Until then, my panties would take the reprieve while they could. I had a feeling I'd be paying up soon enough.

When I got to my car, a certain angel with windblown hair was leaning against it. "What are you doing here?"

"Don't sound so excited," Gabriel grumbled, his lower lip poking out. If I could touch him, I'd bite that lip. God, I needed to get laid.

"Sorry, but I need to get to work." I reached through him, trying to ignore the fact that my hand was practically going through his groin. I started to open my door, but Gabriel shifted until he was almost completely inside of me. Groaning at the tingles rushing through my body, I growled, "Do you mind?"

"Not really." Gabriel grinned, a dimple showing on that right cheek I couldn't help but want to lick.

"Well, it's annoying."

"Is it?" Gabriel chuckled. "From what I smell, it's not annoying you at all."

I pressed my thighs together and cursed my raging hormones. Maybe I'd just get a good vibrator and have a masturbation marathon. I wonder if the guys would want to watch? I know Lucifer would for sure. He seemed the type to be into to that kind of thing, and there was Michael's offer before…

"I can't wait to taste you," Gabriel murmured his thumb stroking the pulse along the side of my neck, the warmth slipping through my skin and straight to my core. "Do you think if I tried, I could kiss you right now?" His mouth descended on mine, and a buzzing brushed along my lips, making my mouth numb.

I jerked my mouth away from him, my hands coming up to push him away, but I only ended up falling through him. I caught myself before I fell on my face. Spinning around, I glowered at Gabriel, who shrugged.

"What?" Gabriel asked.

"How did you think that was a good idea?" I crossed my arms over my chest with a sigh.

Gabriel shrugged again. "You can't blame a guy for trying?"

"I suppose not." Despite my quip, I had been hoping it would work too. I shook my head and sighed. "I promised Mandy I'd be down at the police station soon. I don't think she'll be happy to find out I'm late because I was making out with invisible guys." I shot a look around the parking lot. I'd completely forgotten where we were, that was how absorbed I'd been by him. Thankfully, no one was gawking at the girl tonguing the air, but I didn't trust it would stay that way.

"Let me come with you." Gabriel appeared on the other side of the car before I even got the door open to my side.

Sitting in my seat, I buckled up and turned on the car before turning to him. "Look, I'm all on board for this kissing in exchange for help, but I don't want you or me to get our hopes up."

"Your hopes are up?" Gabriel cocked a brow.

"As are my nips." I shot him a grin. "Believe me

if you could touch me right now, we'd be in the back of my car like a couple of randy teenagers."

Gabriel glanced back at the back seat. "I'd never fit back there."

I laughed. I couldn't help it. These guys were going to be the end of me.

6

Blessed Falls Police Department sat in the center of town, which made a long and awkward ride for Gabriel and me. Or maybe just me. Nothing seemed to bother this guy.

I glanced at Gabriel out of the corner of my eye. His lips were moving along with the song on the radio, and he looked so adorable I couldn't help but smile.

"What?" Gabriel asked.

"Just funny seeing an angel singing Taylor Swift." I kept my eyes on the road so I wouldn't miss my turn.

"She's catchy."

I shook my head and laughed. "Well, I'm sure

Taylor would be happy to know she has fans on Earth and in Heaven."

"Think I could get her autograph?" Gabriel wagged his eyebrows.

"And I'm supposed to what? Somehow approach her as your go-between? No, Miss Swift, the autograph isn't for me, it's for the angels." I snorted. "Yeah, that'd go over well."

"You have a gift. No one ever said it would be an easy thing to bear." Gabriel grinned, but he was barking up the wrong girl. I'd been told by many a people I had a gift, but the problem was none of those were humans. Angels, of course, would want me to see them, who wouldn't? But until humans stopped being judgmental assholes, I didn't see how my so-called 'gift' as a positive. Not unless I was a porn star and needed a bit of fluffing.

"You get to talk to God and all, right?" I asked suddenly. "Maybe you could talk to him for me. Ask him to take it back or make it so I can touch you guys. Cause really, unless everyone else is seeing what I'm seeing, I'm always going to be the weird psychic girl people only want to date so they can say they did it. But if I could touch you guys, at least I'd be getting laid."

"Really?" Gabriel's mouth dropped open

slightly, ignoring the last bit. "People really say that?"

I snorted and put my car in park as we stopped at the police station. "No, I believe the words the guy used was, 'Now I can tell everyone I've fucked a psychic.'" I got out of the car not caring to see the shocked expression that was probably all over Gabriel's face.

Slinging my bag over my shoulder, I kept my eyes forward even as I heard Gabriel's feet on the pavement catching up to me. A cute police officer offered me a smile and opened the door for me as he was leaving. I nodded and grinned in return. Just a normal girl greeting a normal guy.

If only I could be so lucky.

I'd been to the Blessed Falls Police Station before, though never on such good terms. I'd been sixteen and as all teenagers rebelling against my parents.

Let me tell you, no one finds it funny when you break into the school gym and paint the words 'the angels are among us' with a big angel giving you the finger. All it earned me was an even worse reputation at school and a hefty fine from the city. I probably would have ended up in juvie, but my father, being who he was, got the sentenced lowered with the excuse that kids will be kids. Wish that excuse worked all the time.

As it was, no one even paid me any mind as I walked through the station doors and to the reception desk. The noise was almost deafening with everyone hustling about. There was a man handcuffed to a bench, a tattoo of a teardrop below his eye. When he noticed I was looking at him, he glared.

Someone was having a bad day.

"Can I help you?" an impatient voice asked me. More like snarled.

Turning back to the counter, I offered the policewoman sitting there a small smile which she didn't return. Dropping the smile, I explained, "I'm here to see Mandy - I mean Detective Stevenson. She's expecting me."

With a sniff, the policewoman, whose badge read 'Smith,' pointed behind me. "Take a seat, and I'll call her."

I glanced back at the large, menacing man and then back to her with a flabbergasted look. "Really?"

Smith didn't even flinch but turned her back on me to pick up the phone. Seeing as I was dismissed, I cautiously made my way over to the bench.

Taking a seat as far away from the guy as possible, I gave him a nervous smile.

"He does not look happy," Gabriel stated and sat between Mr. Teardrop and me. He leaned close as if to inspect the angry guy's teeth. "This guy is about to get questioned about beating up his ex-girlfriend's new guy. They'll let him go, but then he'll go to her house and kill him."

"Great," I muttered.

"What'd you say?" the soon-to-be killer growled, scowling my way.

"Nothing," I quickly said, crossing one leg over the other as I tried to make myself as small as possible. Mandy needed to hurry it the hell up. I didn't need Gabriel getting visions of every single criminal's future. People already thought I was crazy, I didn't need to add to the mix.

When Mandy appeared, I could have kissed her on the spot, but the moment I saw her frown, my relief changed.

"What's wrong?" I stood from the bench to meet her.

She rubbed a hand over her face and shook her head. "Nothing. The Captain is just busting my balls. Come on. They're back here."

"Why was he busting your balls? You don't have

balls to bust. Shouldn't he be busting someone else's balls?" I followed her through a door that led into a room full of desks.

Instead of laughing like I had been aiming for, Mandy let out an exasperated sigh and stopped at a door that read 'Interview Room 1.' "Please, behave. This is my job, and I'd like to keep it."

"I don't know why," I complained as I backed into the room Mandy led us to. "All you blues seem to have lost your sense of humor."

"It happens at the academy," a deep voice answered, and I spun around to find a middle-aged man with graying hair and a twinkle in his eye. Sitting next to him was another man, but his night-stick was shoved so far up his ass, I could see it coming out his face. Oh, wait that was just his nose.

I smiled at the two as I was ushered by Mandy to the seat opposite of them. "A humor-ectomy, huh?"

"Something like that," the first man smiled. "I'm Captain Welling, and this is Detective O'Connor, Detective Stevenson's partner, who I believe you already know?"

"Know?" I grinned up at her my hands clasped before me. "We go back to when gel pens were still cool."

"Gel pens aren't cool anymore?" Captain Welling asked, his eyes going to Mandy for confirmation. She gave a little shake of her head and then shot me a warning glare.

"Anyway, Mandy - I mean Detective Stevenson" - I grinned up at her, earning me an eye roll - "said you would like my help with a missing person case."

"Well, yes," Captain Welling started but was interrupted by Detective Stick Up His Butt.

"First, we have a few questions for you, regarding your background and abilities." He used air quotes around the word abilities. Someone must have spit in his coffee this morning.

Captain Welling cleared his throat, and Detective O'Connor shifted in his seat his eyes going down to the table. Down, boy. We knew who held the leash in the room now.

"I apologize, Miss Mehr. Some of our police force are having a difficult time believing that people have gifts beyond our understanding."

I restrained from snorting. That was an understatement. "Don't worry about it." I held my hand up and shook my head. "I get it all the time. Some people are just closed off to the mystical world, and that's okay." I offered Detective O'Connor a condescending smile. "I'm sure you are a *great* detective."

Gabriel, who I hadn't noticed coming into the room after us, appeared next to me. He took one look at the unbelieving detective and said, "His wife is divorcing him, and they're going to have dinner tonight to sign the papers."

I made a cooing noise and reached across the table, placing my hand on top of Detective O'Connor's. He didn't seem to know what to do but let me hold onto them for a moment. "I hope your dinner tonight goes well. My friend's parents split up when we were young, so I remember how difficult it had been for him."

Detective O'Connor's eyes widened, his mouth dropping open. As quickly as it happened, his face shut down, and he jerked his hand from mine, glaring up at Mandy. "I'd appreciate it if you didn't tell other people my business, Detective Stevenson."

"I didn't." Mandy's voice went up an octave, and I felt bad.

"Detective O'Connor, Detective Stevenson didn't tell me anything. We hardly speak about work. I didn't even know she had a partner until she mentioned it this morning." I shot her a look, telling her I hadn't forgotten her slip-up. Either I was her best friend or not. Who else was she telling her secrets to? I'd kill them.

Detective O'Connor cleared his throat and tapped his pen on the table. "Fine. Good guess then, but I still don't believe in psychics."

I gave him a pitying look but didn't prod him further. "Whatever makes you comfortable."

"Stop being a spoilsport. We need this woman, so show some respect." The captain clapped Detective O'Connor on the back. At least, someone was on my side.

He flinched at the contact and opened a vanilla folder in front of him. "I have some questions regarding your background, Miss Mehr."

"Sure," I said, leaning back in my chair. "Ask away."

I waited for Detective O'Connor to start his interrogation because there was no way this was anything but that. Gabriel hung out at my side, leaning against the side of the table. His presence was a comfort and a hindrance. If they needed more proof of my abilities, he'd be right there to help me out, but he also made my skin prickle with goosebumps just from his nearness. I tried to stay still so I wouldn't show my discomfort. Cops were very perceptive with those kinds of things.

"Says here that you were arrested for breaking and entering and destruction of public property.

Want to explain that?" Detective O'Connor seemed a bit too excited to see I had a rap sheet.

I shrugged, not letting it bother me. "I was sixteen and rebelling, don't we all?"

Detective O'Connor didn't seem to buy it but continued, "You also graduated from the University of Arizona with a Bachelor's degree in ..." He chuckled and met my eyes. "Religious Studies?"

I shrugged. I seemed to be doing a lot of that. "Seemed like a good idea at the time."

I'd really picked the degree of study to help figure out more about my own abilities. Sadly, the school couldn't tell me anything but the history and theology of all the world religions. I knew more about Buddha and Allah than I did about my own family. The only thing it turned out to be was a waste of my father's money.

"And did you do anything with this degree?" Detective O'Connor asked, grinning like the bird who ate the cat. Or was it the other way around?

"I work at a bar," I sneered. "What do you think?"

"I think we're done here. Captain." Detective O'Connor stood and looked to his superior. "With all due respect, I don't need some delusional crazy woman without a lick of sense messing up my case."

"Now, wait a second," Captain Welling tried to argue, but I jumped in.

"You might want to check your little report again." I gestured to the envelope with a nod. "Along with my Bachelor's in Religious Studies, I also have a Masters in Public Relations and Business. I'm not just some quack looking for a quick buck." I shoved my chair back and leaned across the table, my anger getting the best of me. "You came to me, not the other way around. I'd be happy just to go back to bartending. At least, the jerkwads there are drunk. What's your excuse?"

Mandy gasped and grabbed my arm, but I jerked out of her grasp. I nodded at Captain Welling. "I apologize, Captain, but I won't help someone who can't respect me or my abilities." The captain gave me a grim look as I marched toward the door. I opened it and saw the guy with the teardrop being escorted to the back. Turning back to them, I added, "That guy there is guilty, and if you let him go he's going to kill his ex's new boyfriend. Just thought you should know."

I left their gaping faces in the interview room and stomped through the precinct. Gabriel strolled by my side, not touching me but just being there. I wasn't sure if he was afraid I'd do something stupid or just didn't have anything better to do.

When we finally exited the precinct, I got tired of feeling his eyes on my back. "Well, that went well, huh?" I said, spinning around to look at him.

Without asking, Gabriel wrapped his arms around me. The warm sensation that came from touching them encompassed me, and I could almost feel the pressure of his arms. Or maybe I was only hoping I did. I inhaled his scent, a mixture of sea salt and sunlight. How one could smell like sunlight, I wasn't sure, but it was the only way I could describe it. I let him hold me for a moment, not caring what I looked like to the passing public. I needed comfort and Gabriel was giving it to me.

After a few moments, Gabriel pulled back and looked down at me. "Better?"

I nodded. "Yeah, thank you." I ran a hand through my hair and headed toward my car. Probably shouldn't have this conversation out in the open. When we were safely in my car, I pounded on my steering wheel. "Guys like that piss me off. Like I can't be smart and have special powers. I can only be crazy."

Gabriel nodded in understanding. "I get it, I

do." He placed his hand on top of mine, hovering just above so it didn't go through and stared into my eyes. His green eyes held flecks of gold in them that glinted in the sunlight. I could get lost in eyes like that. "You are smart, beautiful, and funny to boot. A volatile combination for any male, human or angel."

Flushing at his praise, I withdrew my hand from his. I wasn't sure what to say. Compliments weren't really something I got often, so when I did, my brain didn't know how to react. Luckily, my eyes caught the time and saved me from responding.

"Crap, I'm going to be late for work." I raced out of the parking lot like a bat out of hell. Did they have bats in hell? I'd have to ask Lucifer later.

7

―――――

Fridays were the worst. For the normal Monday through Friday workers, this was the start of the weekend, and that meant the bar would be up to its eyeballs with the weekenders.

When I raced through the front door, I was still adjusting my dark locks into a high ponytail. The front door banged behind me, earning me a curious look from Bret.

"I know, I'm late!" I cried, running past him. I'd had enough time to get home and throw on my work clothes before I had to book it out the door. I was lucky I'd remembered my boots, or I'd be leaning over the bar all night, something my back would hate me for by closing.

Rounding the bar, I clocked in at the register just in time for my boss, Bill, to come around the corner. "You're late."

"I know, I know. I'm sorry." I held my hands up in defense.

Bill wasn't the worst boss in the world, but I also wasn't the best employee so I couldn't give him too much grief about it. At least, he didn't try to grab my ass or make me 'come talk about my future.' Thankfully, he was as plain as they came with his business-cut brown hair and IT-guy-shaped glasses. Why he wanted to own a bar was beyond me. He didn't seem the type.

"Why are you late this time?" Bill asked, setting up the rest of the counter's condiments, something I was supposed to do.

"Had to go to the police station." I tried to say it nonchalantly, hoping it didn't sound as bad as it did.

"Police station? For what?" Bill raised a brow at me and leaned against the side of the bar, his slight muffin top hanging over his belt.

Surprised he didn't freak out more, I decided to tell him the truth. "They wanted me to help with a case. My being psychic and all."

"Oh, is that all?" Bill smirked and started

restocking the cups. "I hope you told them you would have to do it around your work schedule."

I wasn't all that sure Bill believed in my abilities. Just like Terry, he was just happy that I made them extra money. Heck, I was happy for the extra dough myself.

I placed my hands on my hips and shifted my weight to one side. "For your information, I told them no."

"No? Why's that?"

I shrugged and shoved my purse under the counter. "I didn't want to juggle my free time playing cops and robbers."

Bill snorted and shook his head. "If I had your abilities, I'd be milking it for all its worth. Talk shows, interviews, even my own book."

"I don't like people," I said, leaving it at that.

"Then you picked the wrong job." Bill turned away from the counter and went into the office as the first few customers came in.

Heavenly Arms didn't have a heavy clientele, so we didn't officially open until five o'clock. Terry and I along with another girl alternated working the bar. This time was my turn to open, Terry would be in later when the after-dinner crowd came in. If it got too busy, Bill would come out and help, but I didn't expect it to get too bad this early.

"Hey, love," Lucifer popped out of nowhere, making me jump. The beer I'd been about to serve sloshed over the side, splashing on my bare legs.

Cursing my choice to wear shorts that day, I sat the cup in front of the customer and grabbed some napkins. Wiping their cup off first, I then turned to my sticky legs.

"Would you like some help with that?" Lucifer purred, leaning against the wall as he leered at me.

"What do you want?" I muttered, kneeling to grab something out of the fridge to hide our conversation.

"Just checking up on you. Contemplating when I will cash in on my payment." Lucifer grinned menacingly.

I returned his grin with one of my own. "Well, that highly depends on you being able to touch me." Lucifer frowned and shifted against the wall. "Based on your expression, I'd say you haven't figured that bit out yet."

"Jane?" Bill's voice made me jump to my feet. The chastising look on his face made me dip my head guiltily.

"There was a … a light out in the fridge. I was just fixing it." I pointed a thumb and kicked the fridge door shut with my foot, so he wouldn't catch my fib.

Bill crossed his arms over his chest, trying not to draw attention to us. Customer service and all. "So, you were talking it back to life?"

Like a deer caught in the headlights, I forced myself to ignore the chuckling coming from Lucifer on the sidelines.

"Oh yeah, I was giving myself a pep talk. You know, good job, you got this. Go, team!" I air punched, just as Mandy walked through the door with Detective O'Connor. Oh great, just what I needed. To Bill, I said, "Oh look, customers! Better go help them 'cause, you know, I'm at work."

I darted down to where Mandy and Detective O'Connor sat, well aware of Bill's eyes on my back. Having my own shop was looking better and better. I wondered if Lucifer would be into that kind of work. I shot a discrete look his way. Today's suit was pressed to perfection as usual and made his legs look long and strong as if he just stepped out of a GQ magazine. He watched the room with a cool, aloof gaze.

It just wasn't fair that someone that gorgeous was the literal Devil. Talk about torture. Just standing there looking the way he did was painful enough to make anyone cry out for mercy.

"Hey, Mandy." I grinned at my bestie and gave Detective Asshole the cold shoulder. "What can I get you?"

Mandy frowned at me and then said, "We're on business, so nothing for me."

"Business?" Glancing up at the clock, it was already half past. "Don't you ever get to go home?"

"Not when people are missing," Detective Asshole snapped, making me finally glance his way.

"Well, I wouldn't want to disrupt your case. So, I'll let you get back to it." I turned to help someone else when Mandy grabbed my arm. I stopped with an irritated huff. "Can I help you?"

"Yes," Mandy's voice pleaded with me. "Detective O'Connor would like to say something to you."

Leaning on my elbow, I waited on Detective O'Connor. His face reddened like a teapot, and I could almost make out the white smoke coming from his ears. This was going to be fun.

"Well, let's hear it, detective. I've got thirsty customers waiting for me." I gestured behind me toward the total of five people in the bar. My comment had the intended effect though. Detective O'Connor's jaw clenched, and his nostrils flared and not in the sexy way the angels' did.

"I might have been a bit rash at my dismissal of your abilities." The utter disdain coming from him as he struggled to get the words out just made me feel all tingling inside. I felt rather than heard Lucifer approach, his body lined up against mine, and I forced myself not to lean into him.

"You're almost as good as one of my torturers." Lucifer chuckled in my ear, a heady sound that made my thighs press together.

Ignoring how the Devil was making me feel, I snapped my fingers in front of the detective. "Come on, detective. Time's a wastin'. Don't want you to be late for your oh-so-important dinner."

A vein in the side of Detective O'Connor's neck throbbed as he bit out. "Please, help us find our missing girl."

"See?" I beamed at him. "That wasn't so hard was it?"

Detective O'Connor snarled at me and barged out of the bar, leaving Mandy on her own. I raised a brow at my bestie. "I hope he isn't like that all the time. I'm not sure how I feel about someone like that watching your back."

Mandy sighed and buried her face in her arms. "He's gotten worse after his divorce started." She glanced up from the table with a sad expression on her face. "He thinks he can still get her back."

"Oh, so it was his fault?" I snorted as I grabbed a rag, pretending to wipe the top of the bar. "I can see that."

"Jane," Mandy warned, her eyes meeting mine. "Please, help us." She sighed once more and sat up straight. "I know your abilities come from the angels, and it's not really you, but could you think about helping us? Just this once? Think about the girl you would be helping?"

Before I could answer, Lucifer chimed in. "Yes, Jane. Just this once. Think of the girl."

What Lucifer really meant was think of the kisses I still owed them if I agreed to help. That stipulation also was heavily reliant on them being able to touch me. So, the likelihood of me actually having to pay up was slim to none. More's the pity.

"I don't know, Mandy." I shook my head, not even pretending to be working anymore. "I have the bar, and I never did get to the grocery store, meaning I have no food in my house now. If that's any indication of how busy this will make me, I don't see how I could do it."

"I'll buy you dinner," Mandy quickly offered, and when I still seemed skeptical, she held up two fingers. "Two dinners! Plus, the precinct will pay you for your time."

My stomach rumbled its vote, and I sighed. "Fine, I'll help you this one time. Then that's it."

Mandy smiled and punched the air. "You won't regret it."

I pointed a finger at her. "It better be a good dinner too. Not some fast food drive-thru."

"Of course, of course." Mandy nodded. "Now, how about a shot? I'm far past due for a break, and that hottie down the bar would look good in my bed tonight."

Shaking my head and laughing, I poured Mandy her usual before making my way to take care of my neglected customers. Lucifer didn't hang around. I kept expecting him to pop in and claim his payment, but he was nowhere to be found.

I finished out the night happy, the case and payment far from my mind as I counted my better-than-normal tips. I even let a drunk guy stay longer than closing, I was in that good of a mood.

"See you later, Terry." I waved to the cowboy

and headed for my car. With no angel in my passenger seat, I made sure to remember my own seatbelt and blared pop music as I sang at the top of my lungs. At two A. M., there were no other cars to make me feel self-conscious about my head banging or out-of-date dance moves. I was usually the one giving drinks, so I didn't get to party much on my own. Plus getting drunk with desire-inducing angels around was not a good idea. I could just see some kind of stripping happening.

Actually, that wasn't such a bad idea. I could have my own private strip club.

Laughing at myself, I pulled up to my apartment and shimmied up the stairs to the beat of the latest tune still stuck in my head. I wandered into my apartment and scanned the area. No angels in sight, I grabbed my phone and dialed the only place open this time of night.

"Mr. Wong's, what can I get for you?" the voice on the other line asked.

"Hey, Todd." I know, Todd for a Chinese name, what are the odds? "It's Jane."

"Jane, my girl. How you doing?" Todd said, sounding more like a homeboy than any Asian descendant. His father, Mr. Wong, was probably having a cow behind him right now.

"Starving," I admitted.

"I got you. You want your usual?" Todd asked. Yes, I order from there that often. If you were a single woman living on her own with weird shifts, you wouldn't be cooking at this time of night either.

"Yeah, that'll do me." Briefly, I remembered my empty fridge. "Actually, can you make that a double order?"

"Got a hot date?" Todd asked, the disappointment in his voice not lost on me.

"No," I chuckled.

"Want one?"

Laughing even harder, I rolled my eyes. "Not right now, but when I do, you'll be the first I call."

"Promise?"

I leaned against the counter in my kitchen and started to answer, but Lucifer caught my eye sitting at my breakfast table. "Would I ever lie to you?"

"For free wontons."

"Okay, you got me. I would do a lot of things for free food." I smiled broadly, earning me a bemused look from Lucifer.

"Good to know." Todd laughed. "I'll have your stuff over in two shakes. Make sure you wear something sexy."

"I'm always sexy," I countered. Lucifer stood

from the table and approached me, my and Todd's line of conversation suddenly making me nervous.

"That you are," Todd agreed and then hung up.

Setting my phone down, I kept my eyes on Lucifer who stalked toward me. "I thought you went home for the night."

"Not before I claim my payment." Those words made my heart race in anticipation. He'd found a way to touch me? Suddenly the Chinese food was not the highlight of my night.

"How are you going to do that?" My voice came out breathless, and my nipples tightened as Lucifer brushed against my front, the tingling sensation shooting straight to my now soaking core.

"I have a theory," Lucifer murmured. "Until this point, we haven't really been trying to touch you, but if I actually put some effort in, perhaps that will change."

I cocked a brow. "So, you're just gonna wish really hard and hope the sex fairies make it come true?"

"Sex fairies?" Lucifer smirked. "No, I'm going to use my energy to focus on touching you."

"So, you're winging it," I countered and then sighed. "I hate to tell you, but Gabriel already beat you to it."

"What?" Lucifer raised his brow.

"Yep," I made a pop with my mouth. "He accosted me in the parking garage right after our meeting. All he did was make my mouth numb."

"Well," Lucifer chuckled. "I'll be damned. Never imagined he'd be so forward."

"You'd know him better than me." I shrugged sadly. "Now, if you don't mind I have a date with the Chinese guy."

"That Todd fellow," Lucifer asked, his grin fading. "Are you having sex with this man?"

"Only when he brings me extra wontons," I deadpanned but quickly corrected myself. "No, he brings me food. We flirt a bit, but that's all. He's not my type."

Lucifer snuggled up closer to me, making my whole right-side buzz. "And what is your type?"

I looked him over, from his perfectly fitted suit to his hand tousled hair. He was the perfect package I would enjoy unwrapping and savoring every taste as I did. Too bad, that wasn't an option.

A part of me wanted to say he was. He, Michael, and Gabriel actually. All three of the heavenly beings made my motor go, go, go like I'd popped a few Adderall. The only problem with them being their all show and no actual follow-through.

Lucifer watched me expectantly waiting for my answer. Before I could answer, there was a knock on my door. Saved by the Chinese.

8

I didn't even remember going to bed that night, but my stomach was yelling at me in the morning. Why did I have to eat *all* the food I'd ordered?

"Fuck me," I groaned, rolling over in bed.

"I'll pass. How about a jelly donut instead?"

Mandy's voice had me popping up faster than a teenage boy watching his first porn.

My eyes fell on the blonde sitting at my tiny kitchen table, a white box and two cups of coffee in front of her. I jumped from the bed, not caring that I was half naked. Apparently, I'd have enough foresight last night to take my pants off before collapsing.

I snatched up the coffee cup and a jelly-filled

donut, scarfing down half of it before I sat down. Hey, I had a stomach ache, but I wasn't dead. "You're a lifesaver," I said with a mouthful of pastry.

"I'm assuming that was a thank you." Mandy laughed, taking a drink from her cup.

I grabbed another donut. "What's the occasion?" I waved a hand at the box and the coffee as I narrowed my eyes. "Don't think this counts as one of my dinners. This hardly even counts as breakfast."

"It's a bribe."

"What now?"

Mandy leaned forward to grab something off the ground. She picked up a file and dropped it on the table in front of me. "The girl who went missing is Clarissa Granes. She's twenty-two and her family is pretty worried."

I glanced down at the file, flipping open the top to see the picture of a blonde woman with a pleasant girl-next-door kind of look to her. "How long has she been missing?"

"About three days." Mandy sighed and pointed at the file. "We've tried everywhere. Her school. Her work. Her friends. No one seems to have any clue where she might have gone."

"Maybe she went on siesta? Took a girl's day. I hear the Bahamas are pretty nice this time of year." My snark earned me a chastising look. I sighed and took another donut. I was going to need a mad workout to make up for these calories. As the cream-filled center touched my tongue, I groaned in pleasure. So worth it.

Mandy made a disgusted noise. "Should I leave you and your donut alone?"

I flipped her off while shoving the rest of it in my mouth. At least the guys weren't here to see me stuff my face. God must really hate me because the instant I thought that, Michael appeared behind Mandy. Choking on my donut, I grabbed my coffee and took a large drink to force the rest of the pastry down. Eyes watering, I coughed out, "Um, what do you need me to do?"

Mandy glanced over her shoulder as if trying to see what I saw. I didn't ask how she knew I saw someone, she'd been around me long enough to know. Still, no matter how hard she looked, the guys never presented themselves to her. It would make my life a hell of a lot easier if they would.

Frowning, Mandy gave up trying to see the angel and turned back to me. "Well, we thought we'd start by having you go back over what we've already done. See if you catch anything we missed."

I was only half paying attention to Mandy, my eyes on Michael as he strolled around my apartment. When he noticed my attire, he raised a brow in question.

Uncrossing and then re-crossing my legs, I tried to make myself think serious thoughts. Not sexy thoughts. No, not the way Michael's jeans fit his ass just so or how his shirt clung to his muscles in such a lickable way. Nope. Not at all.

"Jane?" Mandy said my name and I jerked my eyes back to her. She glanced around the room with furrowed brows, clearly frustrated at her inability to see. "I'm assuming there's an angel here now?"

Forcing myself not to stare at Michael's gorgeous mouth as it tipped up into a smile, I focused on my friend. "Yep. Michael."

"Like the archangel?" Mandy's brows raised.

"Uh ..." I chanced a look at Michael who nodded, bemusement twinkling in his eyes. "Sure. At least, that's what he says. As far as we know, he could be the plumber."

Michael crossed his arms over his massive chest and glowered at me in a way that only upper management could. Being the mature adult I was, I stuck my tongue out at him. Michael's gaze darkened, and he was suddenly leaning over me, his arms caging me in at the table.

"The next time you show your tongue to me, it better be to remit your payment. Otherwise, I will remove it from your person." The dangerous warning in his voice made me shrink into my chair, my tongue furled as far back into my mouth as possible.

"Jane," Mandy said her voice full of alarm. "Is he threatening you? Where is he?" I saw her hand go to the gun on her waist, and I quickly reached out and grabbed her other hand.

"No, it's fine. You can't hurt him anyway." I glared up at Michael and used my other hand to gesture for him to back up. Thankfully, he didn't argue and moved back to give me some breathing room. "Besides, he was just being a jerk. I've had plenty experience handling those."

Michael snorted, but I ignored him.

"If you say so." Mandy settled back in her chair, but her hand didn't leave her weapon.

"I do say so." Dusting my hands off, I stood from my seat. With as much dignity as one could have wearing nothing but tiny panties and a shirt, I grabbed up the first pair of jeans I could find. I could feel Michael's gaze burning a hole in my skin as I pulled them over my legs and hips. I almost didn't change my shirt, not trusting he'd keep his hands to himself, but the stale beer from last night permeated my nose. The top had to go.

Thankfully, I'd left my bra on last night. Strange, since it was usually the first thing I took off when I got home. But with food and a sexy devil distracting me, I guess I could forgive my past self this once.

With a semi-clean shirt on, I grabbed my bag and was ready to go. "Where to, boss?" I smiled cheekily at Mandy.

My bestie had already put the files she'd given me away and was waiting by the door. Michael stood near her, and for a moment I thought she might be able to feel him. Her posture was tense, and her hand hadn't left her gun, but then I realized she was just reacting to before.

"I thought we'd go see Clarissa's parents first. See if you notice anything there. Get a premonition or whatnot."

"Premonitions are Gabriel's thing," I corrected her as we made our way down to her car. "Where's Detective O'Connor? I was so hoping to have the pleasure of working with him."

"Haha," Mandy rolled her eyes, not missing my sarcasm. "He took a personal day, and what do you mean premonitions are Gabriel's thing? They each have a thing?"

"Gabriel has premonitions, Michael is super observant, and Lucifer is like a human lie detector." I ticked them off on my fingers as I named them. "You know, I feel for Detective O'Connor. I'd take a personal day too if I had just signed the love of my life away. Maybe we should send him flowers. Flowers are a divorce thing, right?"

I really did have a moment of empathy for Detective O'Connor. I'd seen the result of divorce. Plenty of the neighbors in my parent's area were divorced. Their kids being caught in the middle of it. I hoped that Detective O'Connor hadn't had any.

"They were separated for a while before now," Mandy informed me as she backed out of the parking lot. "So, it was long coming, but I heard she left him because he worked too much, which sadly comes with the territory."

I punched her on the shoulder and grinned, trying to lighten the mood. "Don't worry, Mandy. I won't divorce you for neglecting me. Not until I get my dinners anyway."

"Thanks for that," she said dryly.

We rode in companionable silence the rest of the way until we pulled into a gated community. You know, one of those neighborhoods that are too good for the rest of the town, so they had to build a wall around them to keep the riff-raff out? Just seeing it made me want to build a pipe bomb and watch it burn.

"Freaking rich people," I muttered to myself, glaring at all the cookie cutter houses that passed by.

Mandy snorted.

"What?"

"Nothing," she shook her head. I stared at her until she finally broke down. I'm that good. "Fine. You're a hypocrite."

"What?" My voice went up an octave. "How am I a hypocrite?"

Mandy gestured around to the massive houses and perfect lawns. "You are hating on people who were virtually you growing up. You lived in a gated community just like this. Your dad has a housekeeper."

"Yeah, my dad," I reminded her. "Not me. I don't make enough to afford a bidet. I don't even have groceries in my fridge."

"That's because you're lazy, not broke." She shook a finger at me. "And you could have a good paying job if you actually used your degree and not do whatever it is you think you are doing."

I hummed. She had a point. While being a bartender let me mess around and avoid being a grownup, it would be nice not to have to worry about money. Maybe consulting with the police was my first step? Gabriel had a promising idea when he said I could get my own shop. I did have a business degree. It could work.

Thoughts of the future swirled in my head, and I didn't even notice we had approached the house until Mandy rang the doorbell. It amazed me what I could do on autopilot. If only I could do everything that way.

"Detective Stevenson," said a man who looked to be in his fifties as he answered the door. He had bags under his eyes behind his thin-framed glasses and a strained look on his face. This had to be the father.

"Hello, Mr. Granes." Mandy offered him a comforting smile. "I called you about coming by with one of our consultants to ask some more questions?"

Mr. Granes's attention moved to me, and he

nodded. "Of course, please come in. I'll just get Janet."

We followed him into the house, and I tried not to gawk. Mandy had been right that my father's house was just as nice as some of the ones in the neighborhood, but Mr. Granes's house made my father's house look like a hobo's hut with the tall ceilings and marble floors. It was all a bit cold and clinical for my comfort though.

"The pictures," Michael's voice brushed my ear. "Check them."

He hadn't ridden in the car with us, choosing to travel however it was angels did. Doing as he said, I searched the pictures on the wall. Like a lot of houses, my family's included, there were the customary family portrait and a few singles around it. I stepped toward them, trying to figure out what exactly I was looking for.

They seemed happy to me. Well, maybe not happy, more like forcibly content. Mr. and Mrs. Granes stood on either side of their daughter Clarissa, their matching outfits of navy blue and white making them look like the perfect little family.

"I don't know what I'm looking at." I glanced at Michael, ignoring Mandy's curious look.

"Yes, what are you looking at?" Detective

O'Connor asked, and I spun around to find him standing in the open doorway.

"I thought you were taking a personal day?" Mandy asked, a bit more rigid now that her partner was there.

"I changed my mind." Detective O'Connor's tone said to leave it alone. I wanted to comment on it, but he didn't give me the chance. "You were saying something about the picture?" He gestured toward the family portrait.

"Uh …" I glanced at Mandy, who shrugged. Suddenly I placed a hand on my forehead my eyes closed tight. "I'm getting something. Something to do with this picture isn't right …" I peeked out of the corner of my eye at Michael.

"Here, his hands," Michael said, coming close to pointing at the picture. My body warmed at the buzzing tingle of him against me, and I tried to focus on what he was talking about and not what he did to me by his nearness.

I closed my eyes again and raised my voice, "His hands! Look at his hands."

Detective O'Connor shoved me out of the way so he could look. "His hands do look a bit wrong. Like they are tightened, almost like he's … holding her in place?"

I met Michael's gaze for confirmation. Michael inclined his head. "That's it! She's not there by choice." My brow furrowed as I turned to Mandy. "What kind of relationship did she have with her parents?"

Mandy's eyes flickered confusion. "Great. Better than most. At least that's what her parents said, and her friends confirmed it."

"Then why is the dad hurting her in this picture?" I pointed a thumb at the one in question. "If they had such a loving relationship?"

"We aren't perfect." Mr. Granes, of course, took that moment to come back in with Mrs. Granes, or Janet, as he'd said. "Detective O'Connor, good to see you." The detective nodded in return before Mr. Granes continued. "That day we had been fighting. Clarissa thought she was too old for family portraits and didn't want to be there." He placed a hand on his wife's shoulder, giving her a reassuring look.

"I see." I drew out, not sure what else to ask. I'd had my fair share of fights with my dad. When I was a teenager, I could drive even the nicest person to drink. My parents were saints for dealing with a kid like me. So, for most parents to have a disagreement with their kid was normal. Healthy even.

Michael didn't seem to like Mr. Granes' answer

though. He passed by me and strolled through the foyer. He seemed to be taking in everything around him like he could see something we couldn't.

"Ask to see her room," Michael commanded, and I repeated the request in a less do-as-I-say tone.

Detective O'Connor made an irritated noise in his throat.

"Are you okay, detective?" I asked, holding up my purse. "Want a lozenge? I'm sure I have one in my bag somewhere."

"No, I want you to stop wasting our time and do your job," Detective O'Connor snapped, putting his hands on his hips, his hand a bit too close to his gun for my comfort.

"I am doing my job, and the spirits require I see her room." I narrowed my gaze at him, daring him to argue.

Mrs. Granes seemed taken back, her hand on her chest as she stared at me. "I'm sorry, who are you again?" She then turned her questioning gaze to Mandy.

Mandy stepped between us. "Mrs. Granes, Jane here is a consultant for our department. She uses an unorthodox method to find things we might have missed. I ask you to please indulge her for a few moments." Her gaze went to Detective O'Connor too, making her partner frown.

Mrs. Granes nodded, still clutching the front of her shirt. "Very well. If you must, but I don't know how you will find anything new. Nothing has changed."

"Thank you." Mandy gave her best professional smile and ushered me up some stairs. I could only assume she remembered the way from last time, but still, it was unsettling to have the parents trailing after us.

When we stopped at a room near the end of the hall, Michael made a comment that made my blood run cold. "The door. Look at those marks."

Discreetly, I tried to search for what he was pointing out. There were scuff marks on the outside of the door and old holes that had been poorly filled in. They'd put a lock on this door.

Mandy opened the door and ushered me in. I stood in the doorway of the missing girl's room with the parents looking in from the outside. Could it get more morbid? Oh wait, it could. The looming angel standing in the middle of the room was just the cherry on top.

I skimmed the room, taking in the lavender bed

set and the desk by the window. Everything was meticulously in its place. Odd.

"I can still feel her presence." I held my hands out in front of me as if feeling something. Good thing I watched a lot of psychic shows or this would have been hard to fake. "Clarissa was living here when she went missing, right?"

I glanced at Mandy and then to the parents who nodded. Something wasn't right here. I smelled a fish, a big, stinky fish that screamed that this bedroom did not belong to a twenty-two-year-old girl. It was too clean. It didn't even look like she had been there. Nothing left out on the desk. No clothes on the floor.

"Did you notice?" Michael asked me, sliding his fingers against the top of the desk.

"Yes, I see," I murmured, turning my back on the parents. Everything seemed to be coming together now. There were things that the parents had left out. Important things.

"What do you see?" Mandy asked quietly, coming close to me. She cast a cautious look to the parents, but I wasn't worried about them. They should be worried about me.

"Yes, what do these all-knowing spirits tell you?"

The sardonic tone in Detective O'Connor's voice irritated me.

"Are you going to question everything I do?" I shot back at him.

"Anything that seems kooky."

"Great," I said, dryly. I turned back to the parents and said, "So, how long did you wait to call the cops before you realized your daughter had run away from home? Was it before or after you removed the locks from her door? Or after you cleaned up her room?" Anger pulsated through me as I asked my questions. How dare they lock up their grown daughter? She's an adult. Old enough to make her own decisions. Live where she wanted. And so what if bartending might not be the most glamorous jobs? It was a living.

Okay, I was projecting now but still, the nerve of them.

"Jane, what are you talking about?" Mandy asked me, surprised by my outburst.

"Yes, I would like to know as well." The fury coloring Mr. Granes voice was not lost on me. Hit a nerve, did I?

Detective O'Connor stepped between us, his hand up to stop Mr. Granes. "I apologize for this. I did not agree to use this person in your daughter's case. But believe me, I will remedy that now." He tried to grab me, but I pushed past him to point at the parents.

"I'm talking about mommy and daddy dearest keeping their daughter hostage. No wonder she ran away." I gestured around the room. "I'd be running from the house screaming myself if I were in her situation."

"Detective," Mr. Granes shouted. "What is the meaning of this? You brought this stranger into our house to make accusations at us when our daughter could be hurt or being held captive somewhere."

"Mr. Granes." Mandy tried to calm him down, but it was Mrs. Granes who broke down.

"You have to understand," Mrs. Granes said between sobs. "Clarissa is a disturbed girl. She needs our protection. She needs us."

"So, you just lock her away? That's your answer?" I yelled at her, her tears not making a dint in my steely gaze.

"That's enough!" Detective O'Connor yelled, trying to grab me again. "These people have been through enough without you making accusations."

"We did what was best for our child. Do you have children?" Mr. Granes growled, and though he couldn't see him, Michael stepped between us.

I'd be grateful for his show of chivalry if anybody else but me could see him. All his move did was block my view. I sighed and waved at his body hoping the contact would make him move.

"I don't, Mr. Granes, but I do know how Clarissa might feel and this." I gestured vigorously. "This is not the answer."

"Get out of my house," Mr. Granes hissed, his breath fogging up his glasses.

"I'll get rid of her." Detective O'Connor grabbed my arm, but I jerked away.

"Gladly," I snapped, stomping passed them. I barreled down the stairs and out of the house. Mandy followed me shortly after, yelling something or another I didn't catch.

"Jane!" Mandy shouted, seizing me by the arm. "Are you even listening to me?"

"No, not really." I shook my head apologetically. "But I'm telling you those people locked her up in that room. Didn't you see the marks from the locks on the door?" I gestured back to the house where Detective O'Connor came charging out.

"What the hell was that?" he shouted at me but to my surprise, Mandy stepped in front of me.

"Leave it alone," she ordered.

"But she just insulted our victim's family. You

can't let her get away with that." Detective O'Connor glared at me.

I flipped him off.

"I can and am," Mandy answered. "The captain asked for her help, and we are going to take it. That means looking at all the other scenarios, and Jane has just brought one to our attention that we would have otherwise never noticed. Now, I'm only going to ask you once, detective. Back the fuck off."

Go, Mandy! I wanted to jump up and down for my bestie but thought better of it.

Detective O'Connor snarled at Mandy but didn't say anything else. He turned on his heel and stomped toward what I could only assume was his car.

When he was gone, I clapped Mandy on the shoulder with a grin. "Way to go, mama."

Mandy nodded. "No one messes with my girl."

9

Normally, I would do anything it took to get out of work. Call in sick, or what not. But tonight, I wanted nothing more than to lose myself in my work.

Perfect for a Saturday night.

The music was booming, and the customers were impatient. Most were drunk before they even got to the bar. I'd had to call Terry to dump ice on a few who were getting handsy already. It was perfect for the mood I was in.

Violence permeated through my veins, and I was just itching for someone to say one more thing to rile me up.

"Hey weirdo!" a familiar voice shouted over the

crowd and a mean smile spread across my lips. Maybe I should wish for a pony next.

Turning to the voice, I took in the annoying chatterbox leaning over the bar. His hair was filled with so much product a match would catch it on fire. He had the typical douchebag attire, colorful, collared shirt adorned with a shell necklace he'd probably gotten at the Gap.

Saddling up to him, I grabbed a rag from the counter. This could get messy. "Hey, Pete. What are you having tonight?"

Pete didn't even try to be discrete as he took in my cleavage and licked his lips. "I'll have a glass of your fine ass."

I chuckled menacingly. "Oh, Pete. You couldn't afford me."

"Oh sure, I could. Besides, who's going to pay for a fucked-up bitch like you?" Pete chugged his glass, laughing the entire time.

As if knowing I needed him, Lucifer appeared. His hands slid around my waist, drawing me closer through the power of tingles alone.

The feel of his presence near my back made me relax slightly, but my anger still pulsated through me. I was almost shaking with it.

"Love," Lucifer purred, his hands moving up and down my sides, making my skin buzz. "You're vibrating with power. I've never felt so much need for vengeance. It's intoxicating."

I wasn't sure what he was talking about and didn't care. I just wanted to beat Pete's face in. Too many witnesses. Can't go to jail.

I forced myself to take a deep breath and let it out. Giving Pete my best kilowatt smile, I said, "You have a nice night, Pete."

I turned away from him, but he caught my wrist in his grip, stopping me. Lucifer growled in response. These guys sure were getting pretty protective of me. Too bad they couldn't help. Damn incorporeal-ness and all.

"Let me go." I locked eyes with the drunken idiot.

"Or what? You'll throw a drink at me? Summon the forces of darkness?" He laughed, looking at the guys sitting on each side of him. They had the good sense not to laugh with him and even tried to move away from him.

"You know," I said with a bitter grin. "Every day of my life, I get crap from creeps like you, and I've had about enough of it. So, why don't you go take your happy self elsewhere? Maybe search for that brain you seem to lack."

The idiot didn't know when to quit. He opened his mouth to spew whatever filth he had concocted. Before he could get a word of it out there, a fist flew through the air and right into his disgusting face.

A round of 'ooh's' and cheers filled the crowd as Terry shook his hand and summoned Bret to throw the asshole out. Grinning at me, the cowboy said, "Man that felt good. Not my hand, but the rest. You okay?"

I nodded, smiling. "Yeah, thanks for having my back."

"Anytime, sweetheart." Terry clapped me on the arm and headed back to his side of the bar.

Lucifer chuckled and tried to brush a piece of hair from my face, which I then did on my own. I turned my back on the bar, glaring at him. "You're no help."

The angel shrugged. "I knew you could handle yourself. Besides, I have the whole not being able to touch anything problem."

"Well, one of these days I might actually need you to be involved. What will you do then?" I fiddled with something by the cash register to hide our conversation.

Leaning up against the wall, Lucifer stroked a finger down the side of my arm, leaving a line of goosebumps in its place. "I guess I'll have to come to your rescue then, won't I?"

"And how will you do that?" I clicked my tongue at him. "Punch your hand in and out of them? You can't deal out any pain unless they are in Hell."

The delicious sound of his laughter caused my body to react. See, I'd decided to wear a backless top today which meant I'd gone without a bra, and my nipples were on full display. At least, I'd worn pants to hide some of my arousal, not that it helped by the way Lucifer was acting.

"Hell's not so bad, especially when you have a friend in charge." Lucifer winked at me before disappearing without a final grope. I had to say I was a bit disappointed. He worked me up so tightly and then left me hanging.

Not fair.

The rest of the night was about the same. By closing time I'd lost count of how many drinks I'd poured and how many I'd dropped on my shoes. These boots were ruined.

By the time the bar closed, my mind only wanted one thing. Sleep. Unfortunately, I wouldn't be able to see my bed for at least another hour. My stomach and my fridge would not let me go one more day on empty.

Stopping at the local grocery store, I would like to say only healthy choices ended up in my basket. But, as I put my items on the conveyor belt, I realized the only thing close to healthy coming from my basket was the strawberry ice cream carton.

The cashier raised a brow as she scanned the five bottles of wine. Standing by my purchases, I shot her a warning look, daring her to question my selection.

"Having a party?" the cashier asked, bagging my third bag of chips. Clearly, I needed to work on my menacing scowls.

"Nope," I said with a pop of my lips. "Just like chips."

"And wine." She nodded to the other bags already back in my basket.

A chuckle came from behind me, and I glanced back to see two teens exchanging looks and not even bothering to hide their laughter at my expense. I gave them my best mom look, which did nothing to deter them.

Since I'd failed at being a responsible adult, I

turned back to the cashier with a cheery grin. "You know what? I lied before, I am having a party."

"Oh yeah?" the cashier asked, her tone of voice saying she didn't believe me.

"Yep, my three big boyfriends are going to come over, and we are going to have an orgy. Drinking wine out of each other's belly buttons and scooping dip off our bodies." I swiped my card to pay for my items and then tapped my chin as if in thought. "Do you think I should put down some towels? I'd hate to ruin the carpet."

The cashier gaped at me, but before she could respond, I grabbed my bags and wagged my fingers at her.

"Wish me luck!"

Chuckling to myself all the way home, I just knew sleep would come easily tonight. Surprising, since the visit to the Granes' and the dick at the bar had drained all my give-a-shits out of my system. Now, I could collapse on my bed and sink into the inky darkness with a grin on my face.

Arms full of groceries, I struggled to flick the light on the wall. A golden hue covered my tiny apartment, and I tensed. I wasn't alone. Still holding my bags, my eyes found the figure lounging on my bed. His suit coat tossed aside, shirt unbuttoned, Lucifer screamed sex and danger.

"If you're here to claim your kiss, you might as well get over it. I'm not in the mood." I set my bags on the counter, a scowl on my face, half upset that I wouldn't get to go to bed and the other half pretending the delectable angel laying there like he'd just stepped out of my naughtiest wet dream wasn't affecting my panties.

Turning my back on the tempting sight, I unpacked my five bottles of wine and array of chips. I sighed in relief when I realized I had indeed bought something more than alcohol and junk food when I found a package of hot dogs. Strange, since I found leftover meat parts forced into a tube utterly horrific.

"Bad night, sweetheart?"

I jumped at Lucifer's voice next to my ear. Standing from the fridge, I glared. "You could say that."

"Well, allow me to make it all better." Lucifer opened his arms to me offering me a full view of his defined abs and the dark trail of hair leading to the top of his pants. My eyes tried to go lower, but I forced them back to his face. I rolled my eyes at the quirk of his lips and twinkle in his dark gaze.

"And how would you do that?" I inclined my head.

"I might not be able to touch you, but I can do other things." He closed in on me until I had no choice but to stare at the hard planes of his chest. His perfect nipples peeking out from beneath his open shirt, taunting me. Desperate for me to slide my tongue along those heavenly pecs.

"Is that so?" I angled my head back to meet his eyes and not my latest obsession. I'd be dreaming of those hard lines tonight, I just knew it. Clearing my throat, I turned back to the counter and grabbed two bottles of the wine, intent on putting them in the fridge. I had a feeling I'd need them sooner rather than later.

"Jane." His deep voice lowered, doing wicked things to my insides. Swallowing thickly, I peered up beneath my lashes, feeling a bit shy in his presence.

That was an unusual feeling for me. Lucifer usually inspired the need to drop my panties, not the feelings of a prepubescent teenager who wasn't sure how to shave her armpits let alone talk to a boy. What was wrong with me today?

I knew what it was.

What happened at the Granes' house had broken through my hard-won shield, the one that helped me keep others at an arm's length. Even Mandy rarely got to peer behind my impermeable defenses, but today had made the fight to keep them up too much. I was tired of it all. I wanted nothing more than to let myself be wrapped up in the arms of someone who cared for me. Wanted me.

Whether Lucifer actually cared for me as more than just a hole to put his hellfire filled horn, I didn't know. The way he looked at me right now said differently. It wasn't just a heat of consuming need, the genuine concern there had me pulling my lower lip between my teeth.

Finally, I sighed. "Why are you here, Lucy?" I used the nickname I knew would break whatever spell had come between.

Lucifer blinked, and the moment was gone. I immediately spun around. I shoved the two bottles into the fridge and shut it with a resounding slam. When I turned back to the fallen angel to see confusion etched on his face.

Tucking his hands into his pockets, Lucifer rocked back on his heels. "Being a friend. Or, at least, I thought I was."

I scoffed as I marched out of the kitchen area. "Our definitions of friendship must be different.

Because most friends don't want to jump each other's bones."

"All the best ones do." Lucifer leered, following me into the living room. "And would it be so bad, Jane? To be my friend. You could use someone like me when your time comes."

Hands on my hips, I glowered. "What makes you think I'm going to Hell? I'm a good person. I don't steal, I haven't murdered anyone, and sure, I do tell the occasional white lie, and maybe I double dip my chips," I explained, crossing my arms over my chest. "But I hardly doubt that's enough to sentence me to eternal damnation."

Like the pain in the butt he was, Lucifer shrugged. Just shrugged. Like that answered everything.

"What was that?" I gestured at him, irritation coloring my voice.

"What?" He cocked his head to the side.

Disbelieving and a bit hysterical, I gestured at him. "That. That shrug." I mimed his shrug back. "When someone asks about their chances of being tortured horribly for the rest of eternity, you don't answer it with a ... with a Goddamn, motherfucking shrug!"

A devilish grin covered his lips. Hands still in his

pockets, Lucifer closed the distance between us. Leaning down, I almost thought he would try to kiss me. My eyelids fluttered in preparation, but his mouth bypassed my lips and brushed against my ear.

"The only one being tortured here is me." After his mystifying words, Lucifer stepped back from me and nodded. "Good night, Jane."

My mouth dropped open like a dog begging for a treat as I stared at the place the angel once stood. What the hell did that mean? He was the one being tortured. Why? Because he couldn't get any? Well, it was a two-way street. I wasn't getting any either!

"Of all the ridiculous …" My voice trailed off as I shook my head. I jerked off my work clothes and pulled on my bedclothes, the entire time thinking of all the different ways I wanted to torture the Devil. Not sexually. No, I meant pulling toenails. Boiling his balls in hot oil. Giving him an at-home perm.

The options were endless.

When I finally dove beneath my covers, I spent the next five minutes muttering to myself and readjusting my pillow. I couldn't get comfortable now. My mind was raging and wouldn't quiet down.

I forced my eyes closed, intent on getting that

good night's sleep like I had planned from the start. Every time I closed my eyes, the flash of Lucifer's concerned expression and the way his lips felt against my skin, even just that tingling buzz, came to mind.

10

———

The next morning, I didn't wake to the smell of coffee and donuts or a sexy angel just waiting to taunt me into a blabbering ball of need. No, for once my apartment was as it should be.

Empty.

Quiet.

I contemplated going back to sleep, making it a lazy day since it was my day off, but then my phone rang.

Of fucking course.

Growling at my utter bad luck, I leaned over the bed and searched the floor for last night's pants. When I didn't find my phone in there, I shoved back the covers and dug through the never-ending pile of clothes. Wasn't there either. The incessant ringing kept going, and I wondered when the hell my voicemail would kick in.

Finally, I stomped across my tiny apartment to where I still had bags of groceries. Suddenly, panic filled me. My ringing phone pushed to the back of my mind, I dug through the bags of chips and dip. I tossed a box of toothpaste onto the floor, and then when I found what I was looking for, I let out a cry of relief.

My ice cream wasn't in the bags! Thank God! I'd still have my chunky strawberry cream cheese ice cream to eat while I binge watched TV today.

While I turned to my freezer just to make double sure my ice cream had made it safely inside despite my distraction with the Devil and his porn star body, my phone had the audacity to start ringing again. This time the sound was closer but kind of muffled. Realization dawned on me.

I whipped the freezer open and found it there sitting on the shelf next to my ice cream. Grabbing the phone off the shelf, I didn't look at the caller I.D. as I swiped it on.

"If you're not the ice cream fairy telling me I can have ice cream for breakfast because I'm an adult and I can make my own damned decisions, you can go screw yourself." I snapped into the receiver.

"I'm sorry, Miss Mehr, but I don't think adults are supposed to have ice cream for breakfast," Captain Welling's voice came through the phone, and I instantly felt embarrassed. "But I promise I won't tell anyone."

"Oh, captain." I mumbled, rubbing my hand over my face. "I didn't know it was you. I'm sorry."

"Don't be." He chuckled. "I have a wife. I know not to come between a woman and her ice cream."

"Uh, yeah." I chuckled nervously. Clearing my throat, I asked, "Did you need something, captain?"

"Ah, yes." A thudding noise came through the phone like the captain had tapped some papers on the table. Did people still do that? Shaking the random thought from my head, I focused on the captain's words. "I was calling to see if you would head down to the civic center. O'Connor and Stevenson are already down there."

"Okay?" I drew out. "What am I doing there?"

"The missing girl went to a therapy group there, and while we already talked to the group we thought —"

"That I could get a read on them," I finished for him. "Sure, but I don't see how that's going to help.

I already told Detective Stevenson that she ran away. Didn't she give you a report?"

The captain coughed and then said, "Of course, of course, but we really should cover all our bases. It couldn't hurt, and if you are right, then we have no reason to worry that she's in any danger."

Dragging a hand through my hair, I stifled a groan. Sure, it'd been fun and would net me some extra money, but I'd thought I'd finished it yesterday.

Unfortunately, as much as my ice cream called to me, I couldn't back out when I'd already agreed to help. Not if I wanted them to think of me for future work, anyway.

Forcing myself to smile so I sounded happier than I felt about it, I said, "I'd be more than happy to make sure we've covered all our bases, captain. I'll head down to the civic center now."

"Thank you, Miss Mehr, I am happy to have you on our team." From the sound of his voice, I believed he actually meant what he said. I didn't think anyone had ever been happy to have me around on their team or not. Not unless there was vodka involved.

I said my goodbyes and started getting ready for what promised to be an even more eventful day. I wasn't sure what to expect at the civic center, but I found I was actually excited to find out.

Throwing on some clothes, a t-shirt with a band logo from my college days, and a pair of jeans - no rips or stains for once! - I was ready to go.

Since I hadn't seen delectable hide nor hair of my angels, I had to assume they'd show up when they were ready to. Until then, I just hoped whatever they needed me for was something I could fake on my own.

Detective O'Connor was waiting outside the civic center when I arrived, looking every bit like he'd swallowed something foul. I searched the area for Mandy but didn't see a lock of her golden head of hair, the traitorous twat. Worse, O'Connor had already seen me so I couldn't hide in my car until she arrived.

Oh, God. He was coming over.

I grabbed the bag of fast food on the passenger seat and pretended to be intrigued with my breakfast burrito. Just as I shoved a big bite into my mouth, Detective O'Connor knocked a knuckle on the window.

Still chomping on my burrito, I lowered my window. "Yes, detective?" I said through a mouthful of food. The look of disgust on his face really warmed my soul.

"Come now, Mehr." Detective O'Connor shook his head. "How old are you?"

Swallowing hard, I smirked. "Well, my birth certificate claims I'm twenty-five, but I feel more of a round number like five."

"Five's not a round number." O'Connor put his hands on his hips, showing off his badge and gun. Oh, detective, what a big gun you have! I kept my comment to myself though. See, I was mature.

"Where's Mandy?" I asked instead, searching the area behind him, hoping God heard my prayers and sent her in to save me.

"Detective Stevenson," O'Connor corrected me with a raise of his thick eyebrows. Really the man needed a wax, those things were lethal. Could poke someone's eye out! Obviously oblivious to the signals his eyebrows were sending me, O'Connor continued, "Stevenson is inside finding out when the meeting ends. The real question is what are you doing here?"

With a smug grin on my lips, I asked, "The captain didn't tell you?"

The unfriendly look on O'Connor's face answered that. Of course, he didn't. I wouldn't tell this dick anything either. Who wants to hear someone bitch at every command given? Not me.

"We don't need you," O'Connor informed me.

"Well, I don't want to be here either, detective," I shook my head with a wry smile. "But sometimes we all have to lay back and think of England."

"What does that even mean?" O'Connor scoffed.

Discarding my burrito, I opened my door, forcing the detective to step back. I clapped him on the arm making him flinch. "It means we are stuck together. So, deal." O'Connor opened his mouth, probably to object when Mandy stepped out of the building and came toward us. Squeezing O'Connor's bicep, I did my best cheerleader impression. "Oh my god, your biceps are huge! You must work out a lot." I nodded my head and hummed my approval. "I can really appreciate a man who takes time to work on his guns."

"Jane," Mandy warned, but she was a day late and a dollar short.

O'Connor jerked his arm from me and stomped past Mandy. "I'm getting a coffee."

Staring after her partner with an exasperated expression, Mandy then set her eyes on me and raised a curious eyebrow. "What did you do now?"

Shrugging, I said, "Nothing. Just being myself."

Mandy smirked. "You just can't help yourself, can you?"

"What can I say?" I held my hands open innocently. "He's an easy target."

My bestie started to say something else but thought better of it. "The meeting Clarissa usually goes to doesn't end for another hour. So, we have some time to kill."

"Sounds good to me. I have a breakfast burrito calling my name." I reached for my car, but Mandy's hand stopped me.

"I have a different idea." The wicked gleam in her eye told me I wasn't going to like whatever she had in mind.

"Whatever it is, no. I woke up hella early on my day off to help you guys. I'm not being subjected to whatever nonsense is going on in your head." I waved a finger at her face.

Grabbing my finger, she dragged me toward the civic center. "Come on. It will be fun. I promise."

Mandy pulled me through the center and down a hallway full of doors. The gray carpet beneath our feet was doing nothing for the beige walls. It was like they wanted to make this place as depressing as possible.

We came to an abrupt halt in front of one of the doors. I tried to read the little piece of paper taped on the wall next to it, but Mandy shoved me inside before I could read it. The carpet and wall coloring followed us into the room. A table sat alone one side of the room with coffee and donuts which I tried to make a beeline for, but Mandy's vice-like grip on my arm kept me in check.

Nails biting into my arm, she led me over to a circle of chairs where a variety of characters had already taken a seat. Mandy sat us down in two of the empty chairs and nodded to a woman across the way.

The woman brushed her strawberry blonde braid over her shoulder and smiled, the freckles on her face making me have a serious urge to play connect the dots. Smoothing her hands over her jeans and too nice of a shirt for this meeting, I knew immediately what she was. "Thank you all for coming. My name is Rosalie, and this is our Imaginary Friends Support Group."

Fuck me.

I glared over at Mandy who kept her eyes forward. She shifted in her seat, proving my laser death eyes were affecting her. That's right, bitch, squirm.

During my internal monologue, Rosalie kept talking, recapping on previous meetings. Watching her, I bet fifty bucks that her name ended with Ph.D. I'd dealt with my fair share of therapists, and if Rosalie wasn't one, I'd eat my underwear.

"We have a visitor today," Rosalie announced, and everyone looked around, me included until her gaze fell on me. Shit. "Please, stand and tell us what brings you here today." She gestured at me as if she could use the Force to make me stand.

Gritting my teeth, I had every intention of staying put just to spite Mandy, but then the sneaky whore reached out lightning fast and pinched me.

"Ow!" I cried out, jumping to my feet. Spinning around, I realized I'd done exactly what I had planned not to do.

Now everyone's eyes were on me like some alien life form of conjoined eyeballs and faces. The sudden imagery of the big blob of a person made me shudder. Talk about too many butt holes.

"Go ahead. Start with your name." Rosalie's soothing voice only made me want to punch her in the vagina. I bet she practiced that voice at home.

"Hi," I started, pausing for a moment to clear my throat, my hands twisting in front of me. "My name's Jane and I ..." I glanced down at my soon-to-be ex-best friend Mandy. The traitor gave me an encouraging nod, and I sighed. Turning back to the room, I gritted out, "I have imaginary friends."

Imaginary, my Aunt Fanny. Just because no one else could see the angels didn't mean they were in my head. Mandy knew they weren't either. So, either she was doing this because she thinks in some twisted way it will help, or she was trying to pay me back for something. What that was, I couldn't put my finger on. I've done plenty of things warranting payback, but who's keeping count?

Mandy, apparently.

A chorus of greetings answered my introduction. Each and every one of them had an eager look on their face as if they were happy to see someone else was as fucked up as they were. Rosalie, the self-proclaimed leader of this bundle of fun, smiled at me like she wasn't already analyzing every word I say.

"Jane," Rosalie shifted closer to the edge of her chair, her hands clasped in front of her. "Why don't you tell us about your friends? What do you think made them first appear?"

"My friends?" I cocked my head to the side as I tried to figure out how to explain my guys. They would be irate to be called just friends. I shot a grin at Mandy, and she tensed, no doubt knowing I was up to no good.

"Well, first off I wouldn't really call them imaginary. They're angels. Like literal angels. Though, they don't have wings. I just assumed that part was something man added. Though I guess I could probably ask them about that, I never really got around to it."

The raised brows and general murmurs around the group told me I was the first to make such a claim. Great. The crazies thought I was crazy. Might as well milk it for all it's worth.

"Also," I kept going, knowing I had the room's full attention. "I wouldn't call them just friends. Maybe friends with benefits. Or maybe even boink buddies. Though, that doesn't seem exactly right either." I tapped my chin with a finger, pretending to think of a better word.

"Wait a second," a guy with a receding hairline and glasses thick enough to be bulletproof held his hand up. "You actually have sex with them? With angels?"

"Of course, she doesn't." A woman sitting next to him shook her head. She had mousy brown hair tied tightly on the top of her head.

"Oh yes, I do," I assured her with a shit-eating grin. Actually, I hadn't, not yet, but they didn't know that. "Let me tell you, they may be angels, but they know their way around the bedroom." I circled my finger in the air. Each of them seemed to lean closer, on the edge of their seats. I hadn't had this much attention since I had been caught making out with Jimmy Blake behind the common area at summer camp.

Overwhelmed with glee, I leaned in as if I were telling a secret, "Like Michael, he has such a filthy mouth, he could get me off just by talking." I fanned myself with my hand, earning me a mixture of curious and horrified expressions.

Dear God, don't let the guys show up now. Talk about embarrassing.

"She's just messing with us." The woman from before glared at me with a sense of self-right-eousness. Funny for someone who was currently sitting in group therapy.

I made a cross over my chest with a smirk. "Swear to God." Really, God had nothing to do with it. He'd probably actually smite me for tainting his precious angels. Though, I had a feeling that happened way before I ever got there.

"So, about these angels." Mr. Receding hairline

seemed even more eager than before to hear my story. "There's more than one?"

"Oh yeah." I nodded vigorously, more than happy to indulge him.

Mandy, on the other hand, did not find me as interesting. She grappled with my hand trying to get me to sit down, but I ignored her. Take that, traitor.

Thinking about my guys always made me hot and bothered, being in a room full of people didn't change that. So, the breathlessness in my voice with my next words wasn't even faked. "For example, Gabriel is wicked hot with his mouth and don't even get me started on Lucifer. I can see why he was kicked out of Heaven. That guy would make any celestial being jealous."

Mandy jumped to her feet. Her hands still gripped tight to my arm, she almost ripped it off as she tried to drag me out of the room.

"I'm really sorry about her. She's off her meds," Mandy apologized, her eyes going to Rosalie who had a curious look on her face.

Therapists. Tell them you see angels and they wanted to write a book about it.

Mandy might be almost a foot taller than me, but I was scrappy. I could hold my own when needed. Wiggling out of her grasp, I held my hands out in front of me with a loopy grin. "I'm talking huge!"

A chorus of gasps responded, but before I could give them an encore, Mandy grabbed the back of my shirt and jerked me out of the room.

Party pooper.

11

My face hurt from smiling so hard. Even Mandy's incessant tapping of her foot couldn't get me down.

"You are unbelievable, you know that?" Mandy scowled at me, but I could see the smile threatening to break out across her face. She leaned against the wall, her arms crossed over her chest as we waited for the group in the room next to us to finish.

Not at all apologetic, I shrugged. "Pretty sure they believed me."

Mandy sighed. "You couldn't be serious for five minutes? Those people could have really helped you."

I snorted. "Do what? Start a collection of animal heads? No thanks."

"That makes no sense." Mandy shook her head. "They are just people. Regular people who have some problems. Like you."

"No," I snapped, taking a step toward her. "They aren't like me. They are randos who have insecurities they use imaginary friends to deal with. I see angels. Real, living, breathing angels. Just because your brain is not wired to see them doesn't mean I'm crazy."

As if things weren't bad enough, not one, not two, but all three of my angels showed up in the tiny hallway. The three hulking angels filled the space around me, their auras buzzing off them and, even in my anger, caused fun tingles between my thighs.

"They're here now, aren't they?" Mandy asked, her eyes searching the area. "Where are they?"

Waving my hand in the middle of Lucifer's chest which was blocking my view of Mandy, I motioned him to move. "Lucifer is right in front of you. Michael's over there." I waved behind me. "And Gabriel's right here." I pointed a finger to my right. To them, I asked, "Why are you here?"

"We can tell when you think about us, remember?" Gabriel smirked. "And you must have been thinking about us hard to get all three of us at once."

"Yes," Michael drawled. "I was in the middle of a debriefing when I felt this tug. What were you doing just now?"

"Yelling at Mandy." I gestured to my best friend who now just looked uncomfortable. I guess I would too if my companion was talking to herself in the middle of the hallway.

Lucifer moved closer to Mandy and poked at her cheek. His finger going through her face was so wrong. Mandy flinched as if she felt him.

"Why were you yelling at her?" Lucifer asked. "Isn't she supposed to be your bosom buddy?"

I snorted and laughed. "Bosom buddy."

"What?" Mandy clipped, her eyes going wide. "You're talking about me, aren't you?"

I shrugged and grinned. "Maybe, maybe not."

Mandy tsked and pretended to stare at her phone. Just like her to be in denial, even when proof stood right in front of her. One of these days, I'd get her to really believe me.

"Did you need us for some reason?" Michael asked, coming around to stand by Lucifer. "Or was your call by accident?"

"Would you believe it was an accident?" I lifted

my shoulders, sheepishly. "But I will need you very soon. I have to go make with the psychic powers and pull some answers from the people in that room." I pointed to a door next to us. The handwritten sign on the door said, "Anxiety and Depression - Ten A.M." Not surprising with parents like Clarissa's to find out she was coming to this particular group.

"I thought we had come to the conclusion that this Clarissa had run away from home?" Michael rubbed his jaw, his eyes inquisitive. "Is she not of age?"

"Sure, but her parents and the cops don't believe me. She has issues." I used air quotes and grimaced. I hated that word. It'd been used to describe me far too many times for my liking by people who didn't know or want to understand why I was different.

"Humans are so judgmental." Gabriel scoffed and shook his head, his blonde hair falling into his face.

"Like you are one to talk," Lucifer pointed out. "There's a reason I'm babysitting Hell."

"Yeah," Gabriel sniffed and brushed his nose with his thumb. "Because you don't know when to sit down and shut up."

"At least, I'm not an ass kisser, Daddy's boy." Lucifer hissed, stepping toward Gabriel.

Michael quickly stepped between the two a stern expression on his face. Seemed like they did this often. "Lucifer, knock it off." Michael's voice boomed through the air making the walls rumble slightly. Even Mandy seemed shocked by it. So, they could affect our world. The little liars.

"What was that?" Her hand went to her gun, her eyes scanning the area.

"That was an angel pissing contest." I frowned at the three of them. "Which, as much fun as it is to see Michael play big brother, we don't have time for." I gestured to the door opening beside us as a few people came out.

Mandy shifted in place, getting her bearings. I could just see the wheels in her head turning as she tried to rationalize the tremor. Humans were so easy to dismiss things they didn't want to believe was true. I wondered how long before Mandy couldn't rationalize it any longer.

Distracted by my thoughts, I didn't see the attacker until a hand landed on my shoulder. Jumping in place, I spun around and raised my hands up in my best karate stance. No, I didn't know karate, but I'd watched enough Jackie Chan movies to fake it. It had worked until now.

Rosalie Group Therapist Ph.D. took a step back, her mouth gaping in surprise. Dropping my hands, I muttered, "Sorry."

"It's quite alright. I should have announced myself." The genuine apology made my knees itch. Why my knees? Who knows? One of those universal questions that never gets answered.

The guys were lingering in the hallway, waiting for me to enter the room. I tried to wave them off, but they weren't budging, the nosey bastards. Crossing my arms over my chest, I turned my attention back to Rosalie. "Did you need something?"

"Oh, yes," Rosalie smoothed her hands over her hair. I wondered if it was her natural hair color. Her coloring really worked with it, but for all I knew, she could be a box dye girl. Not that it mattered, but it was good to know trivial things like that about people. Never know when you needed a good insult. Digging in her purse, Rosalie pulled out a card. "I was hoping you would take a moment to speak with me. Your story really interested me, and I would love to hear more about your condition."

Condition. I huffed. I'd show her a condition all right.

"I don't mean to be rude." Okay, so I did, but adulting required me to say it. "But I don't have any interest in pouring out all the nitty gritty sordid details of my life to you, Rosalie." I drew out her name to make sure she got the full extent of how utterly revolting the idea sounded.

Giving me a tight grin, Rosalie held the card out even more. "Still, if you change your mind."

Sighing, I took the card from her and made a show of putting it in my back pocket where it wouldn't stay longer than it took me to find a trash can. I'd eat it just to be immature, but the guys already had a bad impression of humans, and I didn't need to add my flavor of crazy to the mix.

"Is that all?" I asked, more clipped than polite.

Rosalie nodded, and I turned away from her, but her voice stopped me. "Jane. I really do think I can help you. I won't judge or make fun of you. I truly wish to know more about you and your friends." She paused for a moment and then corrected herself. "I mean lovers. The unknown has always intrigued me."

Shooting daggers at the guys who had matching smug looks on their faces, I waved over my shoulder. "Then go talk to a palm reader. See if she can find your natural color somewhere under all that dye." See? Ammunition for later.

I didn't wait for her to answer before pushing through the guys and into the room, spine-tingling buzzing or not. Most of the people had left already, so there were only a few stragglers inside. Mandy spoke to a tall man with glasses and a bow tie. Really? Who wore bow ties anymore? This wasn't England.

"Jane." Mandy waved me over to where she talked to Mr. Bow Tie. As I approached her, I realized Mr. Bow Tie was actually a grade A hottie. Nerdy but hot. If he had been my therapist, I might have actually stayed. Though, the likelihood that I would take him seriously was slim to none.

Lucifer slipped his arm around my waist, tingles running along my skin as he brushed his fingers along the skin between my shirt and pants.

Clearing my throat as well as my turbulent thoughts, I offered Mr. Bow Tie my hand. "Hi, I'm Jane."

"Me Andrew." Mr. Bow Tie said in a deep voice, his words choppy.

I exchanged a look with Mandy who shrugged. "Uh, nice to meet you, Me Andrew."

Shaking his head, Mr. Bow Tie chuckled. "Sorry, I couldn't help myself."

"I'm sorry?" I raised a brow, not following his line of thought. Was this some kind of therapy humor I wasn't getting? I would think I'd be up on the lingo by now.

"You know, Me Tarzan, you Jane?" Mr. Bow Tie cocked a brow, his hands open wide as he glanced between Mandy and me, begging for us to get his joke. Which I did, unfortunately.

I forced a laugh and pointed a finger at him. "I get it. Good one." Not really. I'd heard that joke a million times, and it baffled me every time.

"My apologies, let me start over. My name is Andrew Marshall. I'm the therapist over this support group." He waved a hand around the room. When I gave him a critical look, he chuckled. "I swear I'm a better therapist than a comedian."

For these people's sake, I hope so.

"Anyway," Mandy, ever the professional, tried to steer the conversation back on point, "Jane is a consultant we brought on to help find Clarissa."

"A consultant?" Andrew really looked me over as if he could discover all my secrets from my clothing choice. Sorry, buddy, no secret to the universe in these pants.

"Yes, I'm a psychic." I forced myself not to smile. No one takes you seriously if you smile when you tell them something absurd.

Andrew smiled, like a 'megawatt my panties would be on fire' smile, or it would be if I weren't already surrounded by hunky man meat. Wow. No wonder so many women came to his group. The curve of his lips would make even the strongest of women pull down their pants and beg for a physical. Okay, he wasn't that kind of doctor, but you get the picture.

"To be honest," - Andrew lowered his voice and leaned forward - "I've always wanted to meet a psychic." He held his hands up in defense and popped that grin of his again. "I know, I know. People in my line of work shouldn't believe in such things but think of how much easier it would be to help people if I could read their minds."

Laughing nervously, I rubbed the back of my neck. "It doesn't really work that way. I can't read your mind any more than I can see through your clothes."

"Can you?" Andrew asked, a cocky smirk on his face.

"Can I what?" I countered.

"See through my clothes?"

Wowzah. This guy. Really. He didn't hold back on the flirting, that was for sure.

I shifted in place, acutely aware of the angels next to me. Lucifer had his hands in his pockets, a smug look on his face as he thoroughly enjoyed my discomfort. Gabriel, on the other hand, frowned, the skin of his forehead bunching up between his eyebrows. Michael, well, who the hell knew what Michael was thinking half the time? Someone would mistake him for a marble statue with how little he expressed himself.

"No, she can't," Mandy answered for me. Go, Mandy!

"Yeah, she's right," I quickly added. "I can't see in your mind or your clothes, but what I can do is find Clarissa. So, why don't we get back to that?"

Frowning, probably a bit disappointed, Andrew nodded. "Of course. I understand. It's horrible that one of my patients is missing like this. I feel so terrible about it."

"No, he doesn't," Lucifer said by my side. I'd had enough practice from the bar to not need to look at him in response, I simply nodded.

I didn't think much of Lucifer's comment. Most people would say they felt bad even if they hated the person. It was expected. If Andrew hadn't said something along those lines, then I'd be worried.

Opening my mouth to ask a question, Michael jumped in. "He's nervous about something. He keeps fiddling with his watch."

My left eye twitched as I restrained myself from snapping at the angel. Really, who was running this show?

"I talked to Clarissa's parents," I explained, hoping to get something from him about what I'd already guessed.

Andrew shook his head, pure anguish in his eyes. "Those poor people. I feel for their loss. I can't imagine how they are feeling right now, not knowing where their daughter is."

"Lie," Lucifer clipped. I held a hand up to stop him and then passed it off as scratching my head.

"So, you didn't know her parents were keeping her hostage." I cocked my head to the side. Did Clarissa open up to her therapist? I know I never did, well, not the way they wanted me to in any case.

Andrew didn't act surprised. In fact, he seemed ashamed. "Yes, I knew about it. Or at least suspected it."

"Dr. Marshall," Mandy stepped in, her brows

furrowed. "You never said anything about this the first time we interviewed you." I could hear the accusation in her voice, and I wanted to know too. Why hold it back?

Andrew sighed and glanced down at the ground. "Doctor-patient privilege. Clarissa doesn't like people to know that her life isn't anything less than perfect."

I snorted. "With parents like hers, I can imagine why."

Mandy shot me a look. Ignoring her, I started to ask my next question, but Lucifer pipped up again. "Ask him where she is."

Since it was a good question, I did as he asked. "Do you know where Clarissa is? Or where she might have gone?"

"One question at a time," Lucifer hissed.

Crap. I forgot. You'd think I'd be a pro at this faking it by now, but I still get caught up on the rules. If I asked more than one question, I made it harder for Lucifer to pinpoint where they were lying.

"No, I have no idea where she is." Andrew kept his hands in his pockets. His face had so much emotion in it I couldn't tell if he was telling the truth or not.

I angled my head to the side, toward Lucifer. It was our signal for him to check. Lucifer stepped toward him so that he was in between our little threesome, his brow furrowed as he studied the man. After a moment, he shook his head.

"He's not telling the truth, but he's not lying." Lucifer turned back to me, frustration on his face. It was almost cute how his inability to figure it out got to him.

Putting my hand to the side of my forehead, I closed my eyes briefly. Making a humming sound in the back of my throat, I waved my other hand in front of Andrew. "I'm sensing you aren't telling us everything, Andrew. You don't know where Clarissa is, but you have an idea."

Opening my eyes, I saw Andrew's brow rise. Shuffling in place, his mouth dropped open. "That's remarkable. How did you know that?"

"So, it's true?" O'Connor asked. I spun around and found the irritating detective behind me, a frown on his face. Man, did this guy ever smile?

"Yes," Andrew quickly answered. "It's true, I don't know where she is, but if she did indeed run away and has not been kidnapped," - he paused as if the thought itself caused him pain - "then there is only one person who might be housing her."

Detective O'Connor stepped into our little circle, his jaw tightened and his gaze intense. How he hadn't been able to crack this guy before baffled me. "Who?"

That one word made Andrew swallow visibly, and he stumbled over his words, "Jack ... Jack Adams. He's a member of our group, or at least was until about two weeks ago."

"Jack Adams?" Mandy scribbled on a little notepad. "Do you have contact information for him?"

Andrew shook his head. "Not on me, but I can send it to you when I get back to my office." He quieted for a moment and then seemed to think of something. His gaze didn't go to the detectives but to me. "He's not a stable guy. If Clarissa is with him, she could be in real trouble."

"Why do you say that?" Mandy asked, her paper poised and ready to take notes. My little honor student. She'd always been the studious type. Never missed a class and her notes were so detailed they were color coded.

Color coded. I know! How did someone so nerdy end up with an awesome, amazing person like me?

"Jack tends to get obsessive. Dangerously so."

Andrew ran a hand over his face and let out a bitter laugh. "Clarissa had always been on his radar, even if he wasn't on hers. But Clarissa seemed to really enjoy having an admirer from afar. Even joked about how it was always good to have a backup. A sure thing, she called it."

"Thank you, Dr. Marshall." Mandy reached out and touched his arm, sympathy in her voice. Andrew smiled weakly at her, placing his hand on top of hers.

O'Connor, on the other hand, didn't seem to feel much of anything for the concerned doctor. Hands on his hips, O'Connor grunted. "Yeah, thanks. You've been a real help."

Liar. Liar. Pants on fire.

As we left the civic center, Gabriel caught up to me. He bumped his hand against mine, his way of holding my hand. My heart pitter-pattered as I stared up into his opulent eyes. Get a grip, Jane!

"That guy isn't going to be of help," Gabriel randomly said.

Glancing at him, I yelled at my heart to knock it off. "Why do you say that?"

I didn't realize my mistake until O'Connor asked, "Say what? I didn't say anything."

Flushing, I muttered, "Nothing, just talking to myself."

Making a disgusted noise, O'Connor increased his speed which wasn't hard with his yardstick legs. With him gone and only Mandy holding back, I waited for Gabriel to answer.

"That guy, Jack Adams." Gabriel shook his head as if he didn't want to say anything. "Man, that guy's dead."

"What?" I screeched. "What do you mean dead?"

"Dead? Who's dead?" Mandy asked, grabbing my arm. I shook her off and waited for Gabriel to explain.

"Find him, and you'll know what I mean." Frustratingly, that's all I got from him before he and the rest of them took off. Ugh. I hated that. Why couldn't they leave like normal people? That way, I could chase after them and demand an explanation. No cryptic messages. No half answers. Just them, me, and a set of kitchen knives.

I was still a bit shook up from Gabriel's revelation about the dead guy, a guy I didn't even know. But being who I am, my mind went to Jack Dawson in Titanic. Another dead Jack to add to the list.

I'll never let go, Jack. I'll never let go. Fuck you, Rose. He could have fit on that door.

Mandy grabbed me again, and I finally turned to her. "Mandy, Jack isn't going to be of help to us. Jack's dead … or will be." I frowned and shook my head. "Still not a hundred percent sure on that part. But find Jack and find him now."

12

———

Finally, back home, I had the day to myself. Or what was left of it. Mandy and Detective Eyebrows were going to search out the dead guy - shudder - and let me know what the next step was.

Not that I didn't have enough on my mind already. Maybe being a consultant wasn't such a good idea. Neither was doing these dishes.

I glared down at the bubbling soap making my fingers all wrinkled and pruny. I really needed to invest in a dishwasher.

Sadly, that requires getting a new apartment, something I was loath to do. I'd been in this tiny apartment since I'd graduated from college. It was all I could afford with what little money I had saved up during my student years. Leaving now would be sad.

But think of the dishes you wouldn't have to wash, a little voice in my head coaxed.

That would be nice. No wrinkly fingers that remind me of old man balls. How did I know what they looked like? Don't ask. Let's just say don't get drunk and Google. You'll find some fucked up shit on the internet.

Once again though, I was back to square one. To have non-wrinkly hands, I would need to get a dishwasher. To get a dishwasher, I needed money. Money I wasn't going to get on a bartender's salary.

You could always do that thing.

What thing?

You know the psychic shop. Find some incense and some bangles, and you're set.

Pfft. I'm not going to do that.

Why not? Could make us some good money. Maybe even better than the bar.

Because it would be ridiculous. I can see myself now, Madame Jane, let me tell your future. No, wait. That's not right. No one would come to see a psychic named Jane. Now, Madame Patrice or Madame Eliza, those are solid psychic names.

I shook my head at my internal monologue,

wondering how I ever thought I was sane. Saving me further insanity, my phone rang.

Mandy.

Wonder if she found Jack yet.

I wiped my soapy hands off on the back of my jeans and grabbed my phone. "What's up, sweet cheeks?"

"Don't call me that." Mandy huffed into the phone. "Can't you answer the phone like an adult? What if I'd been the captain or worse, your father?"

"I do check my I.D. before answering, you know." Besides that one time with the captain earlier this morning but she didn't need to know about that.

"Anyhow," Mandy drew out. I could just see her rolling her eyes, her hand on her hip as she contemplated why we are friends. Believe me, I know. It'd happened before.

"Did you find Jack?"

Mandy sighed, the sound showing how tired she was already.

"I'll take that as a no." I leaned against the counter and crossed my arm under the one holding the phone.

"Doctor Marshall gave us the information he had on file, but it was wrong." No surprise there.

"Luckily, we looked him up in our system, and we have one Jack Adams with priors."

"Oh really?" My brows raised in surprise. So, the guy actually existed. Well, I knew that. Gabriel wouldn't have said what he had if good ol' Jack was made up. I didn't share my doubt with Mandy. Instead, I asked, "Is he our guy? Maybe there's another Jack Adams. It's not a very original name."

"Well …" Clicking followed by tapping made me believe Mandy was on the computer. "He was arrested for assault and stalking. Apparently, he has quite a problem keeping girlfriends. There are five restraining orders against him, all from women."

"So, Jack is more Jack the Ripper kind of Jack and not the Jack Dawson kind of Jack," I muttered, a sinking feeling settling in my stomach.

"He hasn't killed anyone. At least, that we know of." Mandy tapped away on her side of the phone again. "We have an address for him, but it's the same one Doctor Marshall had."

"So, either Jack lied, or he moved," I mused. I had a feeling it was the prior.

"Right. He has his mother listed as his emergency contact, so we're gonna try there and see if we can find him. Maybe you could get with the spirits and find us an address?"

I knew what she really meant. Ask the angels if they can find our missing stalker. I understood Mandy couldn't really say angels in the office. Not with Detective I-Believe-In-Real-Police-Work trailing her ass.

"You need to stop hanging out with O'Connor so much. Your sarcasm is showing."

Mandy snorted. "No, I need to stop hanging out with you. I try to work as little as possible with him. So, if anyone is rubbing off on me, it is you."

"Hey, I resent that," I cried out, placing a hand on my heart as if she had hurt me. She couldn't see it, but the emotion was real. "I could pretend everything is cupcakes and rainbows like you, but I'm aware that those rainbows are just light reflecting off the water and those cupcakes are full of dirt."

"Such a romantic you are." Mandy laughed. "I don't know how some lucky guy hasn't snatched you up yet."

"Well, the celestial cock blockers would be one reason," I grumbled. My vagina made its own cry of distress, demanding I pay attention to it. "I have cobwebs where a penis should be. Sagging boobs where a guy's hands should be holding them up. Seriously, Mandy, I need cuppage!"

Mandy laughed until she snorted like a pig. "You are deranged."

"No, just horny." I quipped back and then as if I had said the magic word, Michael appeared in my living room. "I got to go, one of those spirits you want me to interrogate just showed up."

"Behave," Mandy warned. I could just see her wagging her finger at me through the phone.

"Yes, mom." I hung up and turned my attention to Michael. "What's up?"

Michael either didn't hear me or ignored me. He glanced around my apartment, his eyes searching for something. It was a bit disturbing to see him walking through my couch and table.

"What are you looking for?" I tipped my head to the side my curiosity peeking with every move he made.

"The cock."

My mouth dropped open in surprise, I choked out, "The what?"

Michael finally looked up at me, his face serious as the grave. "You said you have three cocks blocking you, but I don't see any farm animals in here."

Almost fainting from utter humiliation, I stuttered, "There are no chickens in my apartment." I refused to call them cocks in front of him. The very thought of it made my face heat.

Curiosity covered his face, and if I hadn't been wishing for the ground to swallow me whole, I'd think it was cute.

"But I clearly heard you."

"I know," I snapped and then forced myself to calm down. "I know what I said. It was a figure of speech. I don't now, nor will I ever have chickens in my house unless they are fried."

Still seemingly confused but accepting my answer, Michael nodded. "Very well. So, your friend has not found the stalker yet?"

"No, not yet." I turned back to my dishes. I needed something to do other than wonder how much of my conversation with Mandy he'd overheard.

"I will ask Gabriel to see if he can get a clearer picture of where the man died."

I nodded. "I'd appreciate that."

There was silence for a moment, and then I felt his heat against my back causing me to stiffen. With my hands in the cooling water, the warmth of his breath brushed my neck and ear. When did he get so close?

"I have another question," Michael murmured

into my ear, his voice low and gravely. So damn sexy.

"Yeah?" I breathed, my heart palpitating in anticipation. Why am I getting so excited? He could be asking me something completely absurd, and here I am soaking my panties from just the sound of his voice.

Unaware of my inner turmoil, Michael's arms wrapped around me, and before you could say 'hold ya, mama,' he cupped my breast in his large palms. Or well, sort of. He wasn't so much cupping them as holding them where my breasts were.

"W-what are you doing?" I gasped not under-standing why I hadn't shoved him away yet. The tingling in my breasts was causing my nipples to harden and who knew what I'd do when that happened.

His head leaned down, so he was looking over me. "I do not see the sagging you complained about. Am I doing the cuppage right?'

Blinking, I barely focused on what he asked. When I did, my body revolted against me, making my hand slip and pain to radiate through my finger. Michael promptly let go of me, something my breasts cried about, and waved for me to give him my hand.

Blood bubbled from where the single knife I owned had caught me. Grimacing at the sight of blood, I ignored him. "Fuck. I need a band-aid."

Before I could get two steps away, Michael stepped in front of me. "Hold your finger out." I gave him an incredulous look. "Just trust me, Jane."

I did as he asked and in slow motion, I watched as he lifted my hand to his face and slid my finger into his mouth. My jaw dropped open and my eyes glazed in lust as he sucked on the injured finger. Each suck seemed to pulsate through my clit.

I could feel him! And oh my god. He's sucking on my finger. An angel is sucking on my finger!

I tried to calm my inner freak out as Michael removed my finger from his mouth. The irritatingly delicious man seemed unaffected by what he had just done. He seemed almost clinical about the whole thing.

Unfair!

"There you are." Michael lets me take my hand back unaware of the melted puddle of goo I'd become.

Holding my hand like it was some piece of priceless artwork, I stare in awe at the newly healed finger. It was like I'd never been cut!

"You can heal wounds with your mouth?" I

asked, still in disbelief. "What are you a freaking vampire?" Before he could answer, I held my hand up, the one that had gotten hurt. "Am I going to get super powers in this hand now? Like some magical transference?"

"No." Michael deadpanned.

"What about just this finger?" I held up my healed finger. "Like super strength? Or can it text as fast as lightning?" I zipped my finger around the air in front of me making a buzzing noise with my mouth.

"Not in the slightest." Michael rolled his eyes. "Now, if you are done injuring yourself, I will be on my way. I'll send Gabriel back to you if he finds anything."

"Sure, thanks," I said distracted by the awesome powers I could have acquired. After a moment, I glanced up and realized Michael was still there. "I thought you were leaving?"

"I am." Michael huffed. "Or I'm trying to but ... I can't."

"What do you mean you can't?" I stopped looking at my finger long enough to study him. "Why don't you just poof away like you usually do?"

"Don't you think I'm trying?" Michael scowled, clearly frustrated at his dilemma.

Circling around him, I tried to search for some reason why he's stuck. "Maybe you need to recharge or something?"

"I'm not battery operated." The archangel crossed his arms over his chest and growled. "This has never happened to me before."

"Oh, I hear ya." I waved off his annoyance. "One time I was in a hurry for class and my battery died in my car. I spent thirty minutes trying to get a jump. Maybe that's what you need, a jump."

And boy, would I like to jump him! Not in the battery sense. The sexual sense. No, down, girl. See what happens when you get a little bit of boob action and some finger sucking? All reason goes out the window, and you're ready to fuck like it's Mardi Gras.

"For the last time, I'm not a battery." Michael snapped and stomped across the room, clearly a pacer when upset.

What happened next, I wished I'd had a camera for. I really did. I'd have won a million dollars for the best fail of the century, but of course, I was too busy staring at Michael's ass as he walked away and then promptly stumbled over the table. His legs flipped up into the air as he tumbled over the couch and landed with a loud thud on the floor.

My hands came up to cover my mouth. My reaction was a mixture of horror, surprise, and laughter. I ended up letting out a half-scream-laugh that sounded like an animal's cry for help.

Michael wasn't any different. The angel just laid on the floor as I rushed to his side. His eyes were wide with shock, not seeming to know what happened or what to do next.

I was right with him there.

"I knew you guys were lying," were the first words to come out of my mouth. Really, I needed to work on my filter. "Incorporeal, my fine ass."

Michael slowly sat up, his hand going to his head where he winced. "Ow. I didn't lie. We aren't corporeal. In any sense. Only God lets us be solid, and that's only after a weeks' worth of paperwork."

"Well, maybe you're fallen," I suggested.

Michael glared at me, and I instantly wished I could take it back. "Lucifer is fallen and isn't corporeal, so that doesn't even make sense," he countered and started to get to his feet. His muscled bulged and I'd be a liar if I said I didn't drool a little bit at the sight of them.

Michael stood and started to pace again, this

time being sure not to run into the couch. Sadly, my apartment being so small and he being so big, he didn't have much to work with. I should have been worried. An angel having a meltdown could not be good. Not for me. Not for the world.

Had I somehow started the apocalypse?

After what seemed like forever, Michael spun around and pointed a finger at me. "You did this to me."

"Me?" I put my hand to my chest, offended that he would even think I could have anything to do with it. "I don't know how to upgrade my computer let alone turn an angel corporeal."

"Yes, you and your finger." He pointed at the finger he had just moments ago had sucked like a lollipop. The reminder still made my clit twitch.

"Hey, now." I pointed said finger at his chest. "You're the one who was all like, I got this and popped my finger in your mouth. I didn't force you."

Michael stroked his chin in thought, his anger cooling. "It must have been your blood."

"My blood?"

"Yes, all angels can heal each other, but I wasn't sure if I could heal you. I thought since you could feel me, I must be able to heal you. This was a good chance to test that out. It seems like I was correct but unaware of the side effects."

"Side effects? From drinking my blood?" If I wasn't thinking of vampires before, I sure as hell was now. Magic healing, blood with magic powers, sounded like a preteen movie to me.

"The question now ..." Michael paused and then sat down on the couch. Legs spread apart, he leaned on his knees his head hanging down. He smacked his lips and locked eyes with me. "... is how long will it last?"

"Who knows?" I shrugged. I sat down on the couch next to him, his body heat warming me differently than when he was incorporeal.

After a few minutes of thinking so hard my head started to hurt, I asked, "This is the first time you've been corporeal, right?" I beamed up at him. "Then you must have so many things you want to do." I started to get excited at all the things he had to try. "There's this great pizza place down the street you have to try. You can eat, can't you? I mean, you have a solid form now," I poked at his stomach which felt as hard and muscular as it had always looked but somehow touching it just made it different. Hotter.

"I believe I could eat," Michael commented, smiling down at me.

"Then let's go." I jumped to my feet. "There are so many things you need to do before you go back to being all ghostly which, let's be honest, could be any second." I started to grab my purse, but Michael's hand caught me, dragging me back to the couch and into his lap. My hands immediately grabbed hold of his shirt, holding me to him. The smell of him assaulted my nose, making my panties even more uncomfortable.

"Jane," Michael looked down at me, his eyes full of a hunger I had a feeling had nothing to do with pizza. "There's only one thing I'm interested in doing right now."

"Oh yeah?" I laughed hesitantly, trying not to notice the way he felt beneath my hands. "What's that?"

"You."

13

As I stared up into Michael's sky-blue eyes, I had a brain fart. A complete total shut down. A brain dysfunction. Did they have little blue pills for that?

"Do you not wish to 'ride me like a show pony?'" Michael looked down at me in his arms, his fingers curled around my thigh.

"Uh yeah." My face flushed at his question. I had said that, hadn't I? Sounded so much better back then when I didn't have the option to touch him. Now, faced with his hard muscles and delicious scent, my body was on the edge of overdrive.

I stared at the skin beneath the collar of his shirt, my fingers itching to reveal more of it. As if reading my mind, Michael reached out and took my hand in his, pressing it to his chest. I watched in awe as my hand landed on the fuzzy material of his shirt instead of passing through him.

"Touch me," Michael commanded. "I feel we don't have much time."

The reminder that he could turn incorporeal at any moment shook me out of my little impotent spell. Without a word, I shifted until I straddled his lap and ripped my shirt over my head. Michael's eyes dropped down to my bra-clad chest, his hot gaze coloring my skin. Not wanting to lose my upward momentum, I slid my hands underneath the edge of Michael's shirt, lifting it up and spreading my fingers out along the hard planes of his abs.

"Dear baby Jesus," I muttered as I took the perfection of his body. I shook my head, trying not to drool. "It's just not right, it's like you've been photoshopped into perfection."

"Photoshopped?" Michael cocked an eyebrow. "I assure you, every part of me is wholly my own."

"I bet it is." I purred, pulling Michael's shirt up even higher. He became impatient with my gradual revealing of his yumminess and yanked his shirt over his head. Suddenly, I was forced to take in the complete perfection that was the archangel Michael.

It just wasn't fair. Even his nipples were nice, not overly pointy or hairy. I could stare at him all day and be happier than a clam. My soaked panties agreed wholeheartedly.

Michael apparently wasn't as content as I was just to look at him. His hands moved from my waist and trailed up my sides, leaving hot streaks of need running through me. He cupped my breasts through my bra, a curious look on his face. "This is much different than touching you before."

I chuckled. "I would hope so." With a coy grin, I reached behind my back and unsnapped my bra, letting it fall between us. Michael's eyes found my bare breasts, and my nipples hardened at the attention.

Moving my discarded bra aside, Michael returned to my breasts, cupping each one in turn. It took everything in me not to moan out in pleasure. I could tell by his dark gaze that he deeply appreci-ated my bare skin. My eyes flicked down to his lips, and our agreement came back to my mind.

"I believe I owe you a kiss." I peered up at him beneath my lashes, a bit shy but also eager to lock lips with the devastatingly handsome angel.

Michael's eyes lifted from my breasts though his hands still palmed them, making me squirm.

Not waiting for him to answer, I licked my lips and lifted my face up to his. I didn't bother with soft and gentle, we didn't have time for that. Who knew when he'd disappear again? I wanted to take advantage while I could.

I threaded my fingers through his hair, tugging his face closer to me and sliding my tongue along the crease of his lips. Letting go of my breasts, Michael wrapped his arms around me, pulling me even closer to him. At the same time, he opened his mouth to me, pressing his length up to rub against my hot core.

Moaning into his mouth, I used both hands to hold onto him as I shamelessly ground my clit against the front of his pants. The fabric between us made it impossible to get as much friction as I wanted, so with a growl, I stood from his lap - earning me a befuddled look from Michael - and then promptly dropped my pants, dragging my destroyed panties with them.

Instead of sitting back in Michael's lap, I moved over to my bed and sat back on it, gesturing with a hand for Michael to follow. His intense gaze on my nude form, Michael stood from the couch and unbuttoned his pants. He wasted no time dropping them to the floor. If he had underwear, I didn't see it because my eyes instantly locked onto the mammoth cock taunting me.

Long and hard, it bobbed its head at me as Michael approached. My tongue peeked out to wet my lips, and the urge to take him in my mouth was almost overwhelming. I wanted to know what he tasted like. Did angels taste different than humans? More importantly, I wanted to see the ever-composed Michael crying out his release because of me.

"If you keep looking at me that way, I will not last." Michael's husky voice drew my attention away from his cock, and I smirked.

"Maybe that's what I want?"

Michael placed his knee on the bed between my thighs and leaned downward forcing me to lay back. "I would love to explore every inch of you, but I believe since we are on a time limit. We should save that for another time."

Poking my lower lip out, I whimpered, "But-"

Whatever I was going to say was cut off when Michael's knee made contact with my wet slit. Michael ground his leg against me, making me gasp and groan. He leaned over me, his fingers trailing over my collarbone and down to circle my nipple.

He plucking at it until I cried out, "This is hardly fair."

Michael gave me a devastating grin. "I never said it would be." His hand dipped between us, his fingers finding my pulsating bundle of nerves. It didn't take much work for him to have me arching off the bed, stars bursting behind my eyes. "So, responsive," he mumbled. He kept stroking me even as my toes curled and a scream ripped from my throat.

Trying to even the playing field, I searched him out and wrapped my hand around his length, causing him to hiss. I tightened my grip on him, moving it along the silken steel. Michael paused in his assault on me and braced himself on the bed. His face pinched in pleasure was almost as good as his finger on me. Almost but not quite.

"Enough," Michael commanded, causing me to shiver at the desire in his voice. Michael put both legs between mine, pushing up until I lay spread eagle. Swallowing thickly, my heart beat rapidly in anticipation as Michael lined up our centers. The tip of him brushed the entrance to my heat, and I squirmed.

Thankfully, Michael didn't have the same addiction that Lucifer had to teasing and pressed forward, filling and stretching me. One hand gripped the sheets beneath me, and the other clawed at Michael's shoulder. Michael let out a low gurgling moan as he pushed completely inside. My legs wrapped around his waist, drawing him as close as possible, and still, it wasn't enough.

"Move, please," I begged him. That's right, I wasn't too proud to beg. I wanted him. I had since the moment I laid eyes on him and his brothers. Now that I had a chance to have him, I was going to take full advantage.

Michael locked eyes with me, the intense desire in his eyes combined with his cock inside of me was almost enough to set me off again. When he began to move, my breath caught. Pleasure rippled through me, rubbing me so completely I couldn't hold back my voice. I screamed and moaned, I yowled like a cat in heat, anything to make him keep going.

While my core was filled to the brim, the rest of me felt sorely left out. It was one of those moments that made me wish Lucifer and Gabriel were around. I needed more hands.

As if sensing my need, Michael's arm wrapped

around me, lifting me up and pressing his mouth to my neck. He bit and sucked at my skin, while my front rubbed against his, causing a wondrous friction on my nipples. In our new position, I had more leverage and took full control of our movements.

I slammed myself down onto Michael's cock, groaning as he hit the deepest point of me. I moved in a hip thrusting motion so my breasts and clit could brush against him. The combination of being touched in so many places was becoming too much. I could feel my climax coming once more, and I welcomed it.

Months of teasing and foreplay with no release had wound me so tight I had feared I'd never get some relief. Now that I knew my blood could make them whole, I planned on using it to take my fill of them.

Slutty? Maybe. But who was going to judge me? God? The guys had been more than happy to share my attention, I couldn't imagine it would be any different now.

I cried out as Michael took over our movements. He thrust into me so powerfully that all I could do was hold on for dear life. One more strong thrust and I was gone. My head reeled, my legs and arms tightened around him, trapping him against me.

Michael didn't let up though, even while I was careening over the edge. It only made him move faster. His breathing came in rampant spurts, and sweat covered both our bodies, making us slip and slide against each other. By the time Michael grunted out his release, I'd already come down from my high and hit it again. Talk about stamina!

Collapsing on the bed, our breathing was the only sound in the room. Eyes closed, I reveled in the after-sex euphoria. My body felt light, almost like I could float up to the ceiling at any moment. I'd forgotten what it felt like to feel so loose and relaxed. I guess all I needed was a good poke to solve my problems.

"Is it always like this?" Michael asked after a moment, turning beside me.

I peeked open my eyes to look at him, my lids still too heavy to function fully. "Like what?"

"An uncontrollable release of hormones." Michael's brow furrowed, and his lips thinned from pressing them together too tightly.

I stared at him for a moment, trying to figure out what he was asking. Then a horrible idea came to my mind. A horrible, hilarious thought that couldn't possibly be true.

Shooting up in bed, I turned to face him a

wicked grin on my lips. "Michael, were you a virgin?"

Michael's brow rose. "Of course not. I've had sexual contact with several female angels, some of which were at the same time."

I held my hand up, suddenly not so giddy to tease him. "I get it. Angel orgies. But weren't those times the same as this?" I gestured around us.

"No," Michael answered, shaking his head, his sweat-coated hair clinging to his face. "For one, angels do not secrete bodily fluids." He ran his hand down the side of my body, the sweat that had cooled there warming at his touch. "And the females are not so vocal or enthusiastic."

I blushed. "Well, to be fair, I'm not usually so vocal either. I've always been a screamer, but that was excessive even for me." I cocked my head to the side. "What do you mean, not as enthusiastic? Don't they like sex?"

"Sure, they do." Michael mused. "But they pretty much just lay there, while you were taking control of the act." His fingers moved down my side and to my hip, curving over it. "Taking as much as giving."

His words caused hot desire to rush through me once more, and I could think of nothing more than climbing on top of him and showing him how much I enjoyed our workout. With a coy grin, I put a hand on his shoulder and gave him a push. I towered over him, pressing my slick heat along his growing cock.

Rocking against him, I said, "That wasn't taking. I can show you taking. I'll make you scream my name, begging me to let you cum. I like sex, Michael. The only reason I've gone so long without it is because of you and the others, but now that touching you is an option? I plan to make up for all the orgasms you have denied me." I reached between us, lifting my hips to position myself over him. As I sank down on his already thickened cock, I groaned out, "Starting right now."

Michael didn't stop me from riding him. In fact, he only grasped my hips with the barest of touches. But he watched. Oh, did he watch. His eyes moved between my face, my breasts, and where we connected. I didn't know why that made it even hotter, but it did. I pushed against his abs as I rode him, glancing down to watch him move in and out of me every once in a while. The sight was truly erotic.

Just as I was about to reach my peak once more, Michael flipped us over. He slipped out of me just long enough for him to turn me on to my stomach. His arm wrapped around my stomach and lifted my backside and then he pushed inside of me once more. At a teeth-clenching pace, he thrust into me. The angle we were at had him hitting a spot inside of me that was so intense I could hardly breathe, let alone scream.

When I hit my climax this time, I didn't expect it. It hit me so fast and hard that my knees buckled and only Michael's arm kept me upright while he finished with a rumble that vibrated through my spine.

Michael released me, letting me sink into the bed. A boneless feeling overwhelmed me, a stupid grin on my face as Michael leaned down and whispered, "I believe I will be doing the taking from now on."

I waved a lazy hand at him. "You do that."

My eyes started to close when a pounding on my door woke me slightly. I didn't have a chance to answer or even get up before Mandy came bursting in. Wearing jeans, and a blazer over a t-shirt, she stomped into my apartment like she owned the place.

"What the hell, you can't answer your phone?" she yelled, staring down at her own. Without looking up, she turned toward the kitchen area. Searching the counter, she snatched something up in her hand. "Ah hah! I knew your phone wasn't lost and it's even on, so then why aren't you answering —"

Mandy spun around, her words catching in her throat as her eyes found Michael still leaning over me completely naked.

I laughed at the dumbfounded look on her face, causing her to turn her gaze on me. Shifting on the bed, I smiled. "Hey, Mandy. Meet Michael. You know, the archangel."

14

The way Mandy stared at Michael would have been hilarious had he not been as butt naked. I got the drool factor, I really did, but a part of me wanted to lash at her with my blunt nails.

Man, I needed a manicure.

"Mandy," I called her name, grabbing the sheet of my bed and covering myself. "You can stop staring at him now."

My best friend blinked and slowly her gaze moved from Michael to land on me. Her mouth opened and closed, her finger pointing at him. "That's Michael."

"Yes," I told her and then looked at Michael.

"We should get dressed. Mandy's brain is turning to mush the longer your porn star body is visible."

Michael quirked a brow at me and then offered me a hand. I reached up and clasped it. Just as Michael began to pull me up, he disappeared. Or rather he was still there, but my hand went through him causing me to fall back on the bed.

I bounced slightly and scowl. "Of course, it would wear off now."

"It would seem that way," Michael agreed, turning his hands over as he looked them over. He didn't seem at all bothered by his nudity.

"Hey, where'd he go?" Mandy asked, her head swiveling this way and that as she searched for him.

I waved her off and sighed. "Don't bother, he's incorporeal again. Just my luck." I slipped off the bed, ending up right in the middle of Michael, who hadn't backed off. My body buzzed with energy, and I quickly stepped out of him.

Grabbing my shirt off the ground, I dragged it over my head. I started to tug on my discarded underwear when the reminder of what Michael and I had been doing started to slip down my leg.

I started toward the bathroom, bypassing Mandy who still was looking for Michael. Using a washcloth to clean off, I yelled out the door, "You might as well stop looking. You're not going to find him."

"What do you mean?" Mandy hurried toward the bathroom. "He was just here. He couldn't have disappeared into thin air."

I snorted. "Yeah, actually he can and often does." I stepped out of the bathroom and pulled some new underpants on. Grabbing my pants from the floor, I slipped them on and buttoned them.

"That's got to be annoying." Mandy frowned. "How do you keep track of him?"

"He's still over there actually," I nodded over at him, my eyes sliding over his delectably nude form. "And still naked."

Michael glanced down at himself and then tried to pick up his clothing. His brow furrowed as his hand kept going through them. Stalking across the room, I picked up his shirt and handed it to him, but when I tried to let go, it simply fell to the floor.

"Well, that's interesting." I cocked my head to the side and stared down at the shirt, crumpled on the ground.

"What is it?" Mandy asked, coming up beside me, only inches away from Michael's bare ass. Even though she didn't have a clue, it still made the she-beast in me roar.

"Michael can't put his clothes on. It seems that while he turned back all ghostly, his clothes didn't." I gestured up and down his nude body, which caused him to get hard. "Really?" I raised a brow. "You're turned on now?"

Michael smiled slightly. "You seem to have that effect on me." He looked down at his clothes and frowned. "This is an unexpected after-effect."

I furrowed my brow and scratched my head. "Can't you just you know, materialize new clothes or something?" Before the words even finished coming out of my mouth, Michael crossed his muscular arms over his chest and clothing appeared. A gray V-neck sweater and tight jeans that hugged his ass like they were made for him. Which they had been.

"Is this better?" Michael asked in a conde-scending tone.

Pursing my lips, I grunted. "No, not really." Michael's smug grin gave me an idea. "Oh, if you can make new clothes, can you —"

"Jane," Mandy interrupted me. "Can you not talk to him like I'm not in the room?"

My grin fell, and I turned back to my best friend. "I'm sorry, I didn't mean to make you feel left out. You can relay anything you want to say to

Michael through me. I mean, if you have questions or whatever." I smiled brightly.

Mandy shook her head, rubbing a hand on her temple. "No, no. Not that this isn't all fascinating - I'm still not sure that it's not some hallucination - we have other things to worry about."

I clucked my tongue. "Well, if you're hallucinating then I am too."

"That isn't comforting," Mandy said sarcastically. She shifted, putting her hands on her hips, exposing her gun and badge clipped to her hip.

"You're still on duty?" I glanced down at her weaponry. "Don't you ever take a break? It's the weekend."

Mandy rolled her eyes. "Did you forget we are still looking for a missing girl? Which by the way, is the reason I came by." Mandy paused, and I waited for her to explain herself. "We found Jack. Or at least, an address to check out. I was trying to get a hold of you, so you could come along and do your, you know, psychic thing." She wiggled her fingers in the air.

"Oh, okay." I shifted and turned to Michael. "Do you want to come?"

Michael shook his head. "No, I need to check into all this."

"This?" I squinted at him.

Taking a step toward me, Michael reached out and brushed his fingers along the side of my face. I leaned into the tingling wishing his hand was solid once more. When he dropped his hand, I sighed.

"I must find out more about this blood exchange. What does it mean? Can it be done again?" Michael explained. "I will send Gabriel to help you."

I shrugged. "Fine, but don't tell them about us until you find something out. Angels haunting me is already a pain enough, I don't need them waiting around for me to get hurt so they can drink my blood."

"That's how it happened?" Mandy asked, a disgusted look on her face. "He drank your blood? Gross."

I cocked a brow at her and then ignored her completely. "Just don't send Lucifer. You know he'll figure it out right away, and that's all I need."

"I thought you wanted him?" Michael asked, no jealousy in his voice but curiosity.

I flushed. "I do, but he can be an insufferable prick when he wants to be. If he finds out we know how to touch, he'll hound me until I fuck him just so he'll shut his trap."

"Very well," he said, and with that, he was gone.

"What?" Mandy asked, searching around. "What happened? Did he leave?"

"Yeah," I muttered. "He went wherever."

"What was that all about?" Mandy touched my shoulder, and I shrugged it off. "Did you two really ...?" She gestured to the bed and then back to me.

"Yeah, we did." I chuckled. "It was fucking fantastic too." I met Mandy's eyes and smirked. "Remember that guy, the one in college."

"Mister All Weekender?" Mandy asked, a grin spreading across her lips. "He's that good?"

I laughed. "Oh, better. We're talking about stamina here. And ..." I held my hands out in front of me measuring out the approximate size of Michael's hardware.

"Really?" Mandy's eyes widened. "Man, not only are these guys real, but they're well-equipped." She dragged a hand through her hair, which she had let down after the civic center. A thoughtful look crossed her face, and then she asked, "Do you think one of them might want to be my new fuck buddy?"

The violent reaction I had to Mandy's question

caught me off-guard. "No, absolutely not," I shouted, glaring at her.

Mandy's mouth dropped opened, and she took a step backward her hands up in a defensive position. "Jeez, bite my head off. I thought you didn't like these guys."

"I don't," I grumbled. "Okay, maybe a little. Or a whole lot. I don't know. They grow on you, and now that I actually have a chance to get physical with them, it makes it all different, you know?" I turned away from Mandy and searched for my purse. If we were going over to Jack's, I'd need my stuff.

"I understand how you feel." Mandy followed me toward the door after I grabbed my bag. "There's this guy at the office that really pushes my buttons, but there's this magnetism between us that just makes me want to let him bend me over the copy machine and really let me have it."

I quirked a brow at her. "Really? Cliché much?"

Mandy grinned. "What? I like the classics. Shower sex. Office sex. I'm a shove me up against a tree in the middle of the rain kind of girl."

I made a face. "That sounds painful and wet. Not to mention the chance of catching a cold." We exited my apartment, and I locked up before following her down the stairs. "So, where are we heading to? And can we stop and eat first? Celestial sex really works up an appetite."

Mandy shook her head. "You and your stomach." We got in the car, and she sighed, glancing at her phone. "I have to wait for a warrant anyway, in case this Jack guy ends up not cooperating."

"Gonna be hard to cooperate when he's dead," I reminded her, clicking my seatbelt.

"We don't know that for sure." Mandy shot me a look. "Where do you want to eat?"

"Burritos?" I asked and then added, "And we do know for sure, Gabriel said so."

"Fine. He's dead. We don't have an autopsy showing that, so we still have to do it by the book." Mandy pulled out of the driveway and down the street. "Didn't you just have a burrito for breakfast?"

"So?" I shrugged. "I like Mexican. Breakfast or lunch. Besides, I need some alcohol to kill some of this" - I shook my jittery hands - "energy."

"Sure you don't want a cigarette?" Mandy glanced over at me with a smirk.

"Why? Do you have one?"

"No, and that's so bad for your health." Her lip curled in disgust.

"And so is drinking, but we're all gonna die sometime." I lifted a shoulder and dropped it.

Mandy pulled into the Del Macho Taco parking lot. "You know, eating fast food will kill you just as fast as alcohol or tobacco. You're starting to look a little, well, hippy."

"What?" I exclaimed, glancing down at my hips. "I am not." Mandy chuckled, and I glared. "You're evil you know that?"

"Hey, I'm not the one going to pound town with a bunch of angels," Mandy countered as she pointed a finger at me.

"One." I held up a finger. "One angel. I'm going to pound town with one angel."

"For now."

What could I say? She was right. The moment I had the chance to get with Gabriel or Lucifer, I didn't see myself saying no. I didn't think I had the willpower to choose just one of them if it ever came down to it.

Michael had his domineering personality that had me wanting to bend over and say, "Spank me, please." I wanted to be the naughty secretary in his billionaire CEO. Whatever he wanted me to do, I'd do it. Probably why he wore the big angel pants up there. He was used to giving the commands.

Lucifer, on the other hand, could command my panties with one look. That guy had some serious game. I had no doubt if Lucifer were solid, he would have his own harem of women chasing after him. Probably why there were satanic cults. They'd gotten a glimpse of his sexiness, and that was that.

Now, Gabriel was a different story. I didn't see him being the type to need to be in control. He seemed more like the wine and dine kind. Don't get me wrong, Gabriel could perv out with the best of them. The number of times I'd caught him staring at my boobs - I didn't have enough fingers. Nevertheless, Gabriel would be a gentleman about it, I was sure.

"What are we talking about?" Gabriel's voice came from behind me, making me jump in my seat, my hand to my heart.

Turning around, I glared at him. "Don't do that!"

Gabriel gave me a sheepish grin. "Sorry, I thought you were expecting me."

"Is someone back there?" Mandy twisted in her seat to stare in the backseat. "Is Michael back?"

"No," I grumbled. "Gabriel just about gave me a heart attack."

"Gabriel?" Mandy raised a brow. "He's the one who can see the future, right?"

"Yeah," I said at the same time that Gabriel said, "No."

Of course, Mandy didn't hear his answer, and I didn't let him explain more as Mandy pulled up to the drive-thru menu. "I want a number six and a number 12 with no tomatoes and a margarita." Mandy gave me a warning look, and I sighed. "Fine, nix the margarita, but we are getting trashed after this tonight. This is my day off, remember?"

Mandy relayed my order to the little person in the box. Just as we are about to move up in the line, the car fizzled and died.

"What the hell?" Mandy yelled, trying to crank her car again.

I twisted in my seat to see a pouting Gabriel. "Really? You're like a million years old, and you're going to throw a temper tantrum?"

"I'm not a fortune teller. I don't see the future," Gabriel snapped, his large muscular arms crossed over his chest making them bulge. I'd have been drooling had he not been acting like a child. A big sexy man-child.

"Fine, you're not a fortune teller," I quipped with an irritated growl. When he refused to turn the car back on, I turned to Mandy. "Gabriel wants you to know, he's not a fortune teller. He's a …?" I glanced back at him, waving a hand at him.

"A seer."

"A seer?" My brow furrowed, and my head angled to the side. "How's that any different than a fortune teller or a psychic?"

"There's a big difference." Gabriel leaned forward, his hands on each of our headrests. "I don't just see the future, but the past and present too."

"What'd he say?" Mandy asked, giving up on trying the car back on. We were lucky we were the only ones in the drive-thru at the moment.

I repeated back to her what he said.

Mandy's face scrunched up. "So, does that mean if he wanted to, he could see what happened with you and Michael?"

I glared at Mandy, but it was too late.

"What happened with Michael?" Gabriel asked, a curious expression on his face. Before I could open my mouth to make something up, Gabriel had a dazed look in his eyes. Then as soon as it came it changed, his eyes widened, and his mouth dropped open. "Michael was solid?"

"Yeah but —" I started but was cut off again by Gabriel.

"You had sex with Michael!"

My mouth snapped shut and glowered at my best friend. "Thanks a lot."

15

"I don't know how many times I have to say it, but I'm sorry," Mandy complained as I stuffed my face full of Mexican food.

Gabriel had finally turned Mandy's car back on, and we were on our way to the police station, where hopefully we had a warrant to go after Dead Jack.

"It's not her fault." Gabriel leaned forward from the back seat. "You shouldn't let her take all the guilt. It's you after all who was keeping secrets."

I didn't look at him but kept putting food in my mouth. If I couldn't talk, then I didn't have to explain. Which was something Gabriel was trying really hard to get me to do. I didn't know why he didn't just use his seer powers and see what happened. He was the one after all complaining about being lumped in with fortune tellers.

Men.

"You really shouldn't be keeping secrets from them anyway." Mandy glanced my way, but I ignored her, the bean and spicy meat combination my sole focus. "You say you like these guys, but if that were true, wouldn't you want to get with them as soon as you can?"

If I had laser vision, I would use it right now to melt in Mandy's brain. She just didn't know when to stop talking sometimes. What next? She was going to reveal my darkest secrets from high school?

Believe me, if you think my 'four ways with the angels' dream was kinky, what I thought up during my hormonal teen years was way worse. We're talking cartoon porn.

"It's nothing to be ashamed of," Mandy continued, glancing my way every once in a while with her puppy dog eyes, but I would not be swayed! "Plenty of women would kill to get half the attention you get from those guys."

Gabriel laughed in my ear, a sound that made it hard to swallow. I grabbed my drink, sucking as much down through the straw as possible as I tried to talk.

"Just because it's normal doesn't mean you need to tell everyone," I chastised Mandy and then turned my attention to Gabriel. "I wasn't hiding it per se, Michael just wanted to check it out first. Make sure there aren't any drawbacks." Gabriel gave me a disbelieving look. I twisted around all the way and put my hand on top of his, well, more like inside, but you know what I mean. "I'm serious. It would kill me if something happened to you guys just because I wanted a little poke and tickle."

Mandy snorted. "Poke and tickle. What are you, a velvet coat wearing gentleman? Who says that anymore?"

I smacked her on the arm. "I do! And don't interrupt, big mouth." Mandy grumbled to herself, but I focused back on Gabriel. "Besides, you know what would happen if Lucifer found out about this before we knew everything about it."

Gabriel grinned. "He'd push you in front of a pair of scissors if he could." I gave him a pointed look which made him frown. "I can see what you mean." Sighing, Gabriel dragged a hand through his already tousled brown hair. "Fine, I understand, but that doesn't mean I'm not still upset that Michael got there first. I thought we had a connection. We did meet first after all."

"We do," I assured him with a soft smile. "And if it had been you instead of Michael, I would have been just as happy. But promise me you won't hold this against him. I don't want me to come between you guys."

"I promise." Gabriel nodded, his eyes serious for a moment before giving me a lopsided grin. "Besides, did you think millennia of being friends would get destroyed so easily by a human?"

I placed my hand on my chest, pretending to be offended. "Why, I never!"

"A beautiful, gorgeous human who I can't wait to get my mouth on." Gabriel leaned toward me, licking his lips as he gave me his best bedroom eyes.

Little rivulets of desire spread through me and settled between my thighs. The thought of Gabriel's mouth on any part of my body made me wet and achy. I wanted him to touch me as much as I had wanted Michael. I was even willing to open a vein for it.

"Well, play your cards right, and you might just get your wish." I grinned coyly, earning me a dark smirk from Gabriel.

Mandy, on the other hand, did not find my words arousing. She made gagging noises before shoving the car into park before the Blessed Falls

Police Station. "If you two are done eye-fucking each other, we have real work to do."

"Eye fucking?" I giggled. "How do you know we are doing any such thing? We could have been talking about cards or knitting."

Mandy scoffed and pointed at me. "I might not be able to see Gabriel, but I know your horny look anywhere. Remember we were roommates during college? We grew up together. There isn't a look of yours I don't know."

"Oh, yeah. What look am I doing now?" I deadpanned, staring directly at her.

Grinning like a fiend, Mandy said, "The 'you're my best friend in the world, and I love you' look."

"Not even close." I shook my head.

"Come on." Mandy opened her door. "O'Connor is probably blowing a gasket already waiting for us."

"When isn't he?" I asked, getting out of the car. Gabriel appeared behind me, his hands in his short pockets as he strolled by my side.

"Good point." Mandy laughed. "But really, we should get this warrant before someone tips him off."

"No one's going to tip him off," Gabriel said. "He's dead."

I repeated back to Mandy what Gabriel said. Mandy shook her head. "Like I said, proof is needed, not the word of an angel." We walked into the precinct, the office busy even though it was a weekend. Lowering her voice, Mandy pointed at me. "And you need to keep the crazy talk to a minimum. Just because I believe you doesn't mean that everyone else will. You sure as hell know O'Connor won't."

"I won't what?"

Mandy, Gabriel, and I stopped in place as the tall Irish man stood before us. If possible, it seemed like the stick up his ass had been shoved in even further.

That didn't keep me from saying, "Won't be joining that dating site for Jews. You know 'cause you're not Jewish." I cocked my head to the side, "Are you?"

Instead of answering my question, Detective O'Connor glared at Mandy. "I don't think my dating life is any of either of your concerns."

"Of course not," Mandy quickly said with wide innocent eyes. "I would never —"

"By never, she means she'd never think you were into large women." Mandy gasped and tried to cover my mouth, but I quickly darted away. "Not that there's anything wrong with liking bigger women. Everyone needs love. Even guys like you."

At this point, the vein in Detective O'Connor's forehead started to pulsate, and I thought I was one second away from getting him to blow. Sadly, just as he was about to go, the captain came barreling toward us.

"O'Connor, Stevenson." Both the detectives snapped to attention. I exchanged a grin with Gabriel and then copied their movements, half tempted to add a salute to the mix.

"Yes, captain?" Detective O'Connor asked, his face still tinged with anger.

"I have that warrant you requested, and we're good to go." Captain Welling's eyes landed on me, and he smiled. "Miss Mehr, how good to see you. I hear you did wonders in finding us this lead. Excellent job."

I nodded my head and smiled broadly. "It's all in a day's work, captain. But I have to say I couldn't have done it without my girl here … and Detective O'Connor's impressive eyebrows." I glanced toward the detective, pointing at the furry caterpillars nesting above his eyes. "They were crucial in our intimidation tactics."

Captain Welling gave me a curious look and

then nodded at Detective O'Connor. "Well, good work, team. Keep it up. Let's find our victim."

"Yes, sir," Mandy and Detective O'Connor said in unison like it was somehow rehearsed. Must be something they learned in the police academy.

When the Captain walked away, Detective O'Connor spun around and jabbed a finger in my direction, his teeth clenched tight. "You are walking a fine line, Mehr."

I leaned forward slightly, my eyes squinting. "You have something green in your teeth, right there." I pointed to the left side of his canine. There wasn't anything there, but it still made Detective O'Connor reach up and dig his nail in between them, a glower on his face.

Mandy grabbed my arm and dragged me toward the door.

"We're leaving already?" I pouted as Gabriel followed behind me. "But I was two seconds away from making O'Connor go ballistic."

Gabriel chuckled at my side. "You're just as bad as Lucifer. No wonder he's attracted to you."

"Am not," I countered and then grinned. "Okay, maybe a little, but don't you dare tell him."

"My lips are sealed." Gabriel zipped his lips with his fingers.

"Come on, Mandy," I urged, getting into her car. "You have to admit it was funny."

Mandy didn't even crack a smile.

I hadn't seen her this mad since Donny Terman took off on her during homecoming. Of course, I beat the crap out of him later when I found him with his pants around his ankles and Slutty Sally blowing him. Nobody messes with my girl, but me.

Cranking the car, Mandy whipped the car out of its spot and headed down the road. Her hands gripped the wheel until her knuckles were white, her eyes focused intently in front of her.

After a few minutes of silence, she finally blew up, "Do you think this is a game?"

"Well, no —" I tried to say, but she cut me off.

"This is my job. My livelihood," she snarled, shooting a look my way. "You can't just act like that to my partner. You could get me fired." She sped around a corner, throwing me against the door of the car.

"Jeez, Mandy. Slow down. You're gonna get us both killed." I held onto the 'oh, shit' handle above my head. "It wasn't that bad."

"Wasn't that bad?" she screeched, her eyes really looking like a cartoon character, the way the red veins bulged. "You insulted O'Connor's eyebrows in front of the captain."

"He didn't seem bothered," I tried to remind her.

"And you could have gotten me charged with sexual harassment! Talking about O'Connor's preferences in women." She shook her head viciously. "They take that crap seriously, you know. Even from a woman. You can't compliment someone's shoes without getting a lawsuit."

I sighed and stared down at my feet. "I'm sorry, Mandy. I didn't mean to get you in trouble. I'll apologize to O'Connor."

"No," Mandy snapped. "You've done enough damage. Just leave it alone."

"But Mandy —"

"Listen to her, Jane," Gabriel commented from the back.

I glanced back at him to tell him to mind his own business but then saw the seriousness in his face. "Did you have a vision?"

"No," Gabriel said, meeting my eyes. "I just know someone like O'Connor, and you won't win any points apologizing. He'll just take it the wrong way."

Huffing, I collapsed against my chair sinking

down with my arms over my chest. "People are so sensitive nowadays. Can't take a joke."

"No," Mandy said softly after a moment. "They just can't handle your kind of jokes."

"What's that supposed to mean?" I arched a brow, my lips pressed into a thin line.

"I love you, Jane. You know that." Mandy glanced my way before looking back at the road. "But you tend to find people's weaknesses and poke at them. Relentlessly."

"No, I don't," I argued.

"Yes, you do," Mandy countered, and there was an echo.

I twisted around to see Lucifer in the back seat with Gabriel. The two of them filled the whole back seat of Mandy's car. Lucifer had an amused gleam in his eyes, and the one side of his lips tipped up in the corner, making him look particularly wicked.

"When did you get here?" I asked, letting my eyes trail up and down his lounging form.

"About the time your friend here tried to kill you all." Lucifer gestured toward Mandy with a curious look. "And I must agree, pet. You would give me a run for my money in the torture department. Funny thing is you don't even realize you're doing it."

Lucifer chuckled. "That's what makes it so damn sexy."

I gave Lucifer an exasperated look. "It's not sexy to be mean to people. Only the Devil would think so."

Lucifer arched a brow.

Shaking my head, I sighed. "Never mind."

"Who's back there now?" Mandy asked. She had slowed down a bit so that I didn't have to worry about wetting my pants anytime soon. Lucky me, since I was running out of pants as it was.

"Lucifer," I said.

"Is Gabriel still here too?" she asked as she pulled into the parking lot of The Other Side Apartment Complex.

I nodded.

"Good, we could use both of them then." She parked in front of a building, I wasn't sure how she knew which one. Probably had the address from before. O'Connor came in behind us a few minutes later as we were getting out of the car.

"Got the warrant?" Mandy asked O'Connor, she avoided eye contact with him, staring at his chest instead. Man, I'd really stepped over the line.

"Right here," O'Connor answered, holding up

a piece of paper. "We should get moving in case he decides to bolt."

"You didn't tell him?" I glanced at Mandy who didn't look at me. Letting out a huff, I looked at O'Connor. He had a kind of guarded expression. I think it was safe to say he was still mad.

"Tell me what?" O'Connor asked, but before I could open my mouth, he held his hand up. "The next thing out of your mouth better be something useful."

I pressed my lips together tightly and raised my brows. After a moment, I said, "Can I talk now?" O'Connor inclined his head slightly. "I've been telling Mandy here, I mean, Detective Stevenson," - I shook my head - "so weird to call you that. Anyway, this Jack guy isn't going to be taking off or putting up a fight."

Detective O'Connor crossed his arms over his chest his eyes narrowing. "And why is that?"

"Cause he's dead," I said matter-a-fact.

Dropping his arms, Detective O'Connor spun around without commenting and started toward the building. I followed him and Mandy, the guys close on my tail. The fact that they hadn't added their own commentary yet was a miracle.

"You really got to this guy, didn't you?" Lucifer

chuckled, brushing his shoulder against mine. The tingles trailed down my arm, and I had the urge to scratch at it.

I grimaced but didn't elaborate, though I'm sure he was dying to hear all about it. Who said I couldn't learn new tricks? See? Progress.

Thankfully, the apartment we were looking for was on the bottom floor. I had enough stairs going up to my own apartment, my butt didn't need any more of a workout. Really, it wouldn't be fair to womankind.

Detective O'Connor knocked on the door. There was no answer. Knocking again, he said, "Jack Adams, it's the Blessed Falls Police Department. We have a few questions to ask you." Still no answer.

"Maybe he's not home," I commented, my hands behind my back, stifling a grin.

Mandy glared at me. "I checked with Jack's mother. She said he should be here. He's living on disability. Something about getting out of the military because of PTSD."

Detective O'Connor knocked once more and still no answer. "I'm going to get a key from the super."

"You're not just going to kick down the door?" I gestured toward the door with a frown.

Shooting me an exasperated look, Detective O'Connor told Mandy, "I'll be right back. Make sure she doesn't touch anything."

I gasped. "How rude. Like I would mess with an investigation."

Mandy pursed her lips and rolled her eyes. We waited a few minutes for Detective O'Connor to come back. Lucifer and Gabriel leaned against the wall next to me, making the grungy hallway look just a little brighter and a whole lot sexier.

I shifted in place, my hands tucked in my pockets, and I glanced between the two of them. Lucifer caught my gaze and held it, making my toes curl. What happened with Michael was on the tip of my tongue, and I wanted so badly to tell him. The prospect of having both of them really had me anxious and horny.

"Stop that," Mandy said as Detective O'Connor approached with the apartment manager.

"What?" I asked innocently.

"You know what you're doing," Mandy whispered before looking at Detective O'Connor. "All good?"

"Yeah, this is Phil." Detective O'Connor

pointed a thumb back at a short rail-thin guy, who looked so happy to be there on a Sunday. I feel ya, buddy. I feel ya.

We waited for Phil to unlock the door and then followed him in. O'Connor and Mandy went in first, but before I could enter, Mandy called out, "Jane, get in here."

I rushed into the room and stopped right behind them, where, in the middle of the living room, Jack Adams had hung himself.

16

Not to speak badly of the dead, but Jack Adams was a slob. A pizza box stacking. Can collecting. Slob.

Really, would it have hurt this guy to clean up occasionally? I could hardly move in his dingy apartment without stepping on a piece of trash.

I shook my foot free of a fast food wrapper and turned to Mandy.

"Don't say it," Mandy warned, cutting me off before I could even say anything.

I held my hands up, my eyes going wide. "I wasn't going to." Though inside, I was going nah nana nah nah. I did tell her. And tell her. And tell her. But did anyone listen to me? No, I'm just the crazy girl who sees angels.

"How did you know about this?" Detective O'Connor glared at me as if I had strung Jack Adams up with his belt and made him jump off the chair.

I was trying not to look at the guy hanging there. His eyes were bulging from his head, his skin gray. The smell alone made me want to gag. I had only ever seen a dead body at a funeral. This was so not the same.

"This man has been dead for a few days already." Lucifer circled around Jack like a vulture taking in his meal. "His soul has long passed."

I raised a brow at him but didn't comment. I didn't need to ask him how he knew. He was the Devil. Souls were what he dealt with every day.

Turning my attention to the suspicious detective, I said, "I heard it from the beyond."

"From the beyond?" Detective O'Connor scoffed and rubbed his jaw. "As in beyond the grave? Did this Jack Adams speak to you, or did someone else tell you we'd find him dead?"

I shrugged. "I don't always know who is talking to me."

"What a load of —"

"What about now?" Mandy interrupted Detective O'Connor which was good because he was being an ass. "What are they telling you now?" I gave her a questioning look. "We hit a dead end with Jack being dead." Something I had already told you. "Where should we go next?"

I turned away from them and took a deep breath. Stretching my hand out, I moved slowly across the carpeted floor being careful not to trip over the random crap at my feet. I made a humming sound as I searched.

"I'm getting something," I said, my hands touching along the edge of the couch. I peeked an eye open and found Gabriel near the door.

Gabriel's eyes glazed over for a moment, too long for Detective O'Connor apparently.

"Come on now, we don't have all day." I spun around to see him with his hands on his hips, a scowl on his face.

"My powers can't be rushed, detective." I mirrored his posture. "Unless you want some second-hand psychic work? If you want that, I know a good fortune teller who could throw the bones for you."

"Do you think this is a joke?" Detective O'Connor growled, stepping closer until we were mere inches apart. "We are trying to find an inno-cent girl, not play your games."

"Not so innocent," Gabriel said, coming out of his haze. "She's not here. I suggest you talk to the therapist again. He wasn't telling the whole truth."

I turned my head away from the detective, gazing off into the distance as if seeing something. Detective O'Connor tried to speak to me again, but I put my hand up, cutting him off.

"Not here. Not here." I gestured down at the ground. "She's not here. We've been sent on a wild goose chase."

"What do you mean?" Mandy asked, coming up next to us. "You're the one who told us to come here."

I shook my head. "No, I didn't. Dr. Marshall did. He's the one who said Jack was obsessed with Clarissa. I simply provided my insight which, I might add, was ignored." I shot her a chastising look. "Now, I am telling you that we were wrong, and we should take another look at the good doctor. See why he accused Jack."

"This is a waste of time," Detective O'Connor sneered. "We have real detective work to do, not this nonsense."

"And what nonsense is that?" I challenged him. "So far, I'm the only one finding anything out about this girl. You didn't even know her family was keeping her hostage. How were you planning on finding her? If we even should be trying to find her."

"Why wouldn't we?" O'Connor countered. "What have your spirits said to make you think we should call this whole thing off?"

"They," I started, attitude leaking into my voice, "think this whole thing is a bunch of crap. Clarissa isn't missing, she ran away. And for a good reason."

O'Connor's eyes glinted with anger. "And what's that?"

I opened my mouth and closed it. I didn't get my answer out fast enough because O'Connor threw his hands up in the air and laughed.

"Speechless, the psychic is speechless. Oh, but don't worry, I will relay to Clarissa's parents that they can stop worrying because the spirits say their daughter ran away!"

"O'Connor," Mandy snapped and reached out to him, but he jerked away.

"This is your fault. You wanted this freak show in our case, and now we are running around chasing our tails." O'Connor tapped his foot incessantly. Mandy started to protest, but he didn't give her a chance. He threw his hands up again and stomped out of the room, the manager close on his heels.

"I hope this guy dies soon. He is just begging to be tortured." Lucifer glared at O'Connor.

"He's torturing himself enough, I don't think he needs you to help," I rolled my eyes. To Mandy, I said, "That guy is going to have a heart attack if he doesn't watch his blood pressure."

"Yeah, well." Mandy sighed and tugged on the ends of her hair. "He does have a point. This does seem like a lot of work for someone to have run away. None of her friends know where she went, even her therapist is concerned for her. Does that sound like a normal college student running away from home?"

She did have a point. Someone should have known where Clarissa was. For no one, not even her friends, to know? That didn't seem right.

If I planned to run away, I'd have talked to Mandy about it first. Have a backup plan in case, I ended up penniless and stranded on the side of the road. Plus, if I ran away, I'd have to bring her too. Can't leave her out in the wild. Who knew what would happen to her without me?

"What do your angels say?" Mandy glanced

around the room, the dead body of Jack swaying a few feet away.

Wrinkling my nose, I shook my head. "Can we take this discussion outside? It's just too morbid." I waved a hand at Dead Jack.

Mandy slid her eyes over to him. "I need to call him in any way. I doubt O'Connor will do it with the wonderful mood he's in."

I snorted. "You mean, he's not always like this?"

Mandy and I moved out of the apartment closing the door behind us. Lucifer and Gabriel didn't follow. Probably off doing angel things. Maybe a communal bath where they scrub each other's backs? I shook the fantasy from my head before I started to drool.

"To be honest, he's actually a pretty cool guy when he's not being ripped in half by his ex-wife." Mandy pulled out her phone and dialed a number. Putting it to her ear, she said, "This is Detective Stevenson, I have a ten-fifty-six. We need forensics and a cleanup crew. Make sure the coroner is called too. Yeah, okay." Mandy rambled off the address and then hung up. "You can go on home, I'm going to wait for the others to get here. Don't want someone to mess with the crime scene before forensics gets to it."

"Why?" I peeked back at the door to Dead Jack's apartment. "Don't you think it was a suicide?"

Mandy nodded. "It looks like it, but we have to cover everything." She let out a frustrated sigh. "Just what I needed though, adding a suicide on top of a missing person's case. With my luck, it's murder, and I'm going to have overtime coming out of my ass."

"Can't someone else take the case?"

"No, because it's tied in with my missing person. Why waste resources?" she sounded like she was quoting someone, probably the captain.

"Well, I'm going to the bar. I need a drink after all this." I waved a hand back at the apartment. "You come by if you get off?"

"If I can, but don't hold your breath."

I waved her off and started toward the parking lot. I got halfway there and stopped in my tracks. Turning back, I walked back over to Mandy who was playing on her phone. "I just remembered, you drove."

Leaning off the wall, Mandy dug her keys out of her pocket. "Fine. I'm sure manager can make sure no one touches the room. I'll be right back."

It only took a few minutes before Mandy was

back. She gestured toward her car with her hand. "Come on, mooch. Let's get you home so you can get drunk."

"Thanks, you're the best!" I looped my arm through hers and skipped to the car.

"You have problems, you know that?" She angled her head toward me.

I shrugged. "No one's perfect."

Mandy and I drove back to my house, both of us lost in our own thoughts. I wasn't sure what Mandy was thinking about, probably the case. She was the definition of a workaholic. Her longest relationship was with her job - or well me, but I wasn't sleeping with her. I mean not that I wouldn't if I was into women. She's hot. You know for someone with a vagina.

I chuckled to myself, earning me a curious look from Mandy.

"What's so funny?"

"If you were gay, would you date me?" I asked, suddenly wanting to know.

"No."

I mock gasped. "What? What do you mean no? I'm a freaking catch."

Mandy shook her head. "You're too high maintenance."

"What?"

"And you are a pig," Mandy continued. "Not to mention, your obsession with naked mole rats."

I scowled. "Hey, they are adorable."

"Also, you're kind of an alcoholic."

"Am not," I argued and then paused. "Actually, I kind of am. But if you had sexy angels giving you a lady boner every other minute, you'd need to be heavily medicated too."

"But you get to have sex with them now." Mandy waggled her eyebrows at me suggestively. "So, no reason to drink now. Why don't you do that instead of going out?"

I snorted. "Like opening a vein just so I can get laid is better than alcohol poisoning."

"Well, you tell me. You said Michael was pretty world rocking." Mandy pulled into my parking lot and stopped the car. "I'm just saying, you've been complaining about not getting any for a while now. This is your chance to get them out of your system."

Pursing my lips, I stared at the dash. "I'm not sure I want them out of my system."

"Really?" Mandy's voice raised in pitch, making my ears ring. "Because I would think guys that hot wouldn't be that interesting out of bed."

"That's so biased." I gave her a really long look. "No, it's not."

"Yeah huh. People can be hot and interesting. Look at me." I gestured at myself. "Look at you." I waved a hand at her. "Are you saying we aren't interesting because we're hot?"

"No," Mandy scoffed. "But you have to admit that Michael is like supermodel hot. Like he's had a sex tape leaked hot."

"I'd watch that," I interjected.

"You know it," Mandy smirked. "Anyway, I'm just saying. I don't want you to get your hopes up with these guys. Maybe keep it casual. Just sex. They're angels after all. What kind of long-term can you have?"

I frowned as I got out of her car. She had a point. Didn't mean I had to like it, though. I had no problem with having tons of sex with the guys. After all, I'd wanted to get with all of them for a while now. The problem was that since I couldn't have sex with them, I'd been forced to get to know them, and it was a bit hard to backtrack to just sex.

Closing the door to my apartment, I sagged against the door. Most of my day was over, and I still hadn't gotten paid for any of the police work. I'd have to talk to Mandy about that.

Heading to the bathroom, I turned on the shower and stripped down. After quickly washing my hair and body, I brushed my toe against my calf. Probably should shave. Then again, I could just wear jeans. But I could end up having sex again with Michael. He didn't seem to mind my prickly legs the first time.

Frowning down at myself, I grabbed my razor. Putting my foot up on the side of the tub, I dragged the razor over my soaped-up leg.

"Did you find out anything?" Gabriel popped up out of nowhere outside the shower curtain, making me jump.

"Ouch, son of a bitch." I stared down at my leg where I had nicked myself. Blood trickled down from the cut and yanked the shower curtain open, glaring at Gabriel.

"Sorry," Gabriel grumbled.

I almost started to yell at him about jumping out of nowhere, but then I glanced back down at the blood and then back to Gabriel.

"What?"

Licking my suddenly dry lips, I said, "Michael tasted my blood."

Gabriel gave me an odd look. "Why did he do that?"

"To heal it." I said, and then blurted out, "it's what made him corporeal."

His eyes widened and then his eyes dipped down to where the blood had started to dry. Kneeling on the ground of my bathroom, Gabriel's eyes stayed on my leg. My heart beat faster the closer he came to me.

Unlike when Michael who had put my entire finger in his mouth, Gabriel's tongue darted out. A tingly feeling slid along my leg where the blood dripped, and then it changed. Warm, wet, and strangely sensual, Gabriel's tongue became corporeal. His lips skimmed against my shin, and I gasped.

Gabriel glanced up from my leg, heat in his eyes as his hand came up and grasped my ankle. A feral grin on his lips, Gabriel growled, "My turn."

17

I didn't hesitate like with Michael. No chit chatting about what he wanted to do now that he was corporeal, though I did know that Gabriel was the more likely of the three to want to indulge in our human ways.

Reaching out, I tangled my hands in Gabriel's hair and let him lift me out of the tub. I wrapped my wet naked body around him as our mouths collided. Gabriel palmed my ass as our lips sucked and nipped at each other, grinding my core against his stomach.

I licked his lips, demanding him to let me in. Opening his mouth, his warm slick tongue pillaged my mouth, searching out my tongue and tugging it with his. I moaned as he sucked on it, pulling at things low inside of me.

"Clothes, too many," I gasped, jerking my mouth away. I curled my fingers into his shirt, trying to take it off. Gabriel leaned away from me long enough to let me drag the offending article over his head. I trailed my fingers along the hard expansion of his chest, the feel of his bare skin against my clit making my blood burn with need.

Gabriel turned us around, pushing me up against the wall of the bathroom. My hand reached up, trying to find something to hold on to, but in the process ended up knocking a bunch of crap off the one shelf in my tiny bathroom. My head bounced off the wall, and I winced.

Pulling my mouth away from Gabriel, I rubbed the back of my head. "Ouch."

"Are you alright?" Gabriel asked, his hand searched for where I hit it. "Did I hurt you?"

"No," I shook my head. "I hurt myself." I sighed and shifted against Gabriel, causing a delightful friction that made me close my eyes for a moment.

"Maybe we should move this somewhere else?" Gabriel grinned at me. "Like maybe the bed."

Chewing on my lower lip, I wrapped my arms around his neck. "I could get behind that."

"Oh, I think I'll be the one getting behind something." The smoldering look he gave me made my breath catch before I started to giggle as Gabriel carried me out of the bathroom. Capturing his mouth again, I rocked against him, his rock-hard abs hitting my slit in all the right places.

We paused briefly when Gabriel pressed me against the kitchen counter. Lifting me up onto it, Gabriel spread my thighs open wide. Giving me a peck and nip, he released my mouth with a wicked grin.

My head fell back as Gabriel dipped down between my thighs. I slid my fingers into his hair, my eyes rolled back in my head as he flattened his tongue against my folds. He lapped at me a few times before pulling my clit into his mouth. I tugged on his hair as the intensity of his mouth over-whelmed me.

Legs wrapping tightly around his shoulders, I arched my hips into him. Gabriel's hands gripped my inner thighs to keep me from crushing his head closer to me. His fingers trailed up and down along my skin, sending rivulets of desire toward my center.

Just moments before I came, my cell phone rang. I tried to ignore it, to keep reaching for my peak, but it kept ringing insistently. My eyes flew open, and I scrambled for my phone on the counter without breaking the contact with Gabriel.

Mandy, of course. The cockblocking ho.

I pushed ignore, but she only called me again. Growling out my frustration, I answered this time. "What?"

Gabriel peeked up from between my thighs, and I urged him back down. He smirked at me and circled his tongue around my clit, making me gasp.

"Why didn't you answer?" Mandy complained from her side. I winced and then whimpered as Gabriel slid a finger inside of me.

"I'm busy," I gasped, swallowing thickly. "What do you want?"

Mandy paused for a moment and then said, "We got a hold of Dr. Marshall. He's in his office now and waiting for us to come meet him."

"Okay," I said, and then covered my mouth to muffle my groan. Gabriel had added a finger and was pumping them in and out of me, his tongue still attacking my pulsating bundle of nerves.

"Well, are you going to come?"

I hoped so.

"I'm …" I trailed off as I let out a silent scream, my body shuddering beneath Gabriel's ministrations.

"Jane?" Mandy asked, worry in her voice. "Are you okay?"

"F-fine," I stuttered and then yanked at Gabriel's head, but he refused to let me come. He lazily stroked me, his eyes peering up at me. The sight alone was erotic enough to get me off. If Mandy would stop talking!

"Jane, are you drunk?" Mandy chuckled. "I knew you said you were going to get trashed, but I didn't expect it to be so soon. I've only been gone half an hour. What'd you do, chug the whole bottle?"

"Mandy!" I shouted just as Gabriel curled his fingers inside of me.

"Oh my god," Mandy gasped. "You're having sex, aren't you?"

"Trying to!"

"Then why did you pick up the phone, you idiot?" Mandy screeched back.

"Because you wouldn't stop calling." Gabriel picked up the speed, making my heart race. I tried to hold back my sounds, but a squeak slipped through.

"Ugh, just meet me at his office when you're done. I'll text you the address." She hung up without waiting for my response. Good for me too because my orgasm was back, and Gabriel finally let me have it.

I dug my nails into his scalp, my phone clutched in my other hand as I cried out. Gabriel released my legs and stood to his feet, licking the remnants of me off his fingers. I was two seconds from demanding he take his pants off when my phone chirped.

Letting out a frustrating groan, I glared down at it.

"Meet me at 24th and Center. And hurry it up!"

Frowning, I turned back to Gabriel.

"What's wrong?" Gabriel returned my frown. "You reached your climax, didn't you?"

I nodded and patted him on the shoulder. "Yeah, it was great but sadly duty calls." My eyes scanned over Gabriel's form, settling on the bulged in his pants. "It's too bad 'cause I really wanted to return the favor."

"That's okay," Gabriel moved back toward me, sliding his arms around my waist. "You can owe me one."

"I think that would be several actually." I

beamed up at him, wrapping my arms around him. He smiled and pressed his lips to mine, and before long we were grunting and groping again.

Of course, just as I started to undo his pants, my phone chirped again.

"Fucking Mandy," I growled, looking down at the screen.

"Ten minutes or I'm coming to get you."

Gabriel chuckled, a sexy sound that made me want to risk Mandy walking in on us. It wouldn't be the first time she'd seen me naked with one of the angels, and it would serve her right.

"Let's go before your friend has a heart attack." Gabriel helped me off the counter and went in search of his shirt while I pulled on new clothes.

"You don't have to come, you know," I told him as we headed for the door. "I'm sure you want to check out some stuff while you can actually feel."

Gabriel shrugged. "The only thing I'm interested in is you ... and maybe one of those burritos you had earlier. They looked good."

Grinning at him, I headed down the stairs toward my car. "I think we can make a pit stop on the way. Michael lasted about an hour before he went all ghostly again. You've got at least forty minutes. Just long enough to get some yummy burrito goodness in you."

I got into my side of the car and waited for Gabriel to follow, but he stood outside the car door, a cute quizzical look on his face. Trying not to grin, I leaned over and opened the door for him. "Come on, can't poof yourself in here anymore."

Gabriel awkwardly got into the car. He shifted in his seat, his brow crinkled. "It's strange."

"What is?"

"Feeling."

"What, you never felt anything before?"

Gabriel shook his head. "It's not the same. Everything is so hard and cold. How do you deal with it?"

"With alcohol and Mexican food," I cracked, earning me a frown. Oh, he was serious. "I don't know," I sighed. "You get used to it. Sometimes, you find someone who makes things just a little less hard and a bit warmer. Then living in this world isn't so bad."

"Do you have someone like that?" Gabriel asked, a vulnerable look on his face.

"Not yet," I smiled softly. I turned on the car, and my car beeped at Gabriel to buckle up. "Put your seatbelt on."

"What?" He glanced at me.

I reached over Gabriel and grabbed the seatbelt. Our breaths mingled, and I paused, realizing how close we were together. The temptation to close the distance between us was overwhelming.

Shaking my head, I broke whatever spell going on between us and clicked his belt in place. Settling back into my seat, I took a deep breath and let it out. Putting the car into drive, I sighed. "Here we go."

We drove down the street for a while in silence, the tension in the car was palpable. I hit a particularly hard bump in the road, and Gabriel's head hit the ceiling.

"Ow." He rubbed his head. "What was that?"

"That was pain. Apparently now, you can feel it too. All the more reason to have your seatbelt on." I eyed the belt across his chest.

"You think I could die?" Gabriel quirked a brow, not at all as concerned as he should be.

Lifting a shoulder and then dropping it, I said, "I don't pretend to know anything about you guys, I just see you. You're the ones with angelic genetics. I'm just saying you should be careful until you know more."

Gabriel chuckled.

"What?" I glanced his way.

"I just find it funny, you telling me to be careful, but you are the least careful person I know." He grinned until I could see his tonsils if I wanted to.

I pulled into the drive-thru of Del Macho Taco and said, "I don't have a death wish if that's what you are saying, but I believe we only have one life. What's the use of playing it safe?"

"But I should?" Gabriel arched a brow.

Stopping at the drive-thru box, I ignored the little voice coming from it and said to Gabriel, "I'm human. I've already come to terms with my imminent death, but you're an angel. Who knows if you dying would start the apocalypse?" I turned away from Gabriel and answered the box, "Can I get three Macho Burritos?" I shot a grin at Gabriel before adding, "And lots of fire sauce."

"Will that be all?" the voice asked.

"That'll do me," I replied and after the voice told me my total drove around the side of the building.

"What's fire sauce?" Gabriel asked, a suspicious look in his eyes.

"Just wait. You'll see." I gave him a coy grin.

When I got to the window, I paid the person and then thanked them as they gave me my food. I handed Gabriel the bag with a large grin. "Bon Appetit."

I drove out of the parking lot while Gabriel dug into the bag. He pulled out one of the burritos, his eyebrows raised as he turned over the metallic paper covered bundle.

"Go ahead," I urged him. "They don't get better as they cool off, believe me, I know." I kept looking over at Gabriel as I started toward the address Mandy sent me. The first bite he took, he made a face, a sort of grimace mixed with awe. A strange expression to be sure.

"So? Do you like it?"

Gabriel's jaw moved up and down, and then he swallowed. Tilting his head to the side, he stared down at it. "I'm not sure. The texture in my mouth is peculiar. Is it supposed to be like that?"

"Like what?"

"Like it's somehow solid but also mushy and … juicy?" Gabriel gave me a look as if asking for confirmation.

I couldn't help it. I laughed. "It's because of all the different ingredients in it." When Gabriel only looked at the burrito like it was some kind of nuclear bomb, I sighed and grumbled, "Maybe we should have started with something easier. Like a chip. Can't go wrong with a chip. It's a fried potato."

"What about this?" Gabriel held up the little container of red sauce from the bag.

"That's the fire sauce." I nodded to him. I parked in the parking lot of the office building Dr. Marshall's office was located. Turning the car off, I grabbed the container from Gabriel and popped the top off. I gestured to Gabriel to hand me his burrito. Pouring some of the sauce on the top of it, I handed it back to him.

Gabriel looked at it, his brows furrowed an intense studious look on his face. I bumped the hand holding the burrito toward his mouth. "Go ahead, try it."

Without questioning me, he put it in his mouth and took a big bite. I reached a hand out to stop him and then covered my mouth, hiding my grin. *I'm a horrible, horrible person.*

At first, Gabriel didn't react. He moved the bite around in his mouth, his eyes narrowed as if expecting something. Then it happened. His eyes widened, and his mouth dropped open. He grabbed at his mouth as if he could stop the burning heat I was sure he was feeling.

"Hot, it's hot." Gabriel turned to me his eyes watering.

I grabbed him as he started to flail about. "It's okay. It's just the sauce. In a second, it'll cool off."

Gabriel waved a hand at his gaping mouth and swallowed repeatedly. Eventually, he calmed down and then looked at me. "You tricked me. You knew that would happen."

"Sorry." I gave him a guilty look. "I thought it better to let you figure it out on your own."

He stared at me for a moment and then down at the burrito. "So, that's fire sauce."

"Yes?" I arched a brow, expecting him to get mad at me. When he took another bite, my mouth dropped open.

"It's not bad." He shot me a grin, and the sight of his cheeks full of burrito made me laugh.

"Yeah, it's not bad."

As we got out of the car and started toward the building, Gabriel said, "We should try this on Lucifer."

Oh God, I've created a monster.

18

———

Mandy and Detective O'Connor were waiting for us in Dr. Marshall's office when we arrived. Stepping into the room, it was exactly like every other therapist's office I've ever been in.

He had a wall full of books. I could bet that Dr. Marshall probably hadn't read most them. He had a globe, that wasn't surprising, and neither were the random pieces of art on the walls. They all looked like they cost more than I made in a year. My eyes skittered over the leather couch that didn't look at all comfortable.

Dr. Marshall might seem like a nice guy, but I didn't see anyone wanting to open up to him. Who could relax on a couch like that?

"What's he doing here?" Detective O'Connor asked, making me look away from the couch.

I glanced at Gabriel and then back to the detective. I opened my mouth to answer as Mandy answered for me. "That's her assistant."

"Assistant?" O'Connor raised a bushy brow. "Psychics have assistants?" He then turned his attention to Gabriel, sizing him up.

Gabriel wasn't even bothered. His crossed his arms over his chest, his floral Hawaiian shirt stretching across his muscles. While O'Connor was intimidating in his own way, Gabriel had almost a foot on him, which seemed to make O'Connor stand even taller.

"This is Gabriel." I gestured a hand toward him, giving Mandy a knowing look. "He helps me channel the spirit world."

O'Connor pursed his lips like he wanted to object to him being there but then didn't. He turned back to Dr. Marshall, who sat behind his desk looking confused at the whole ordeal. Not wanting to linger on Gabriel's presence any longer, I stepped up to Dr. Marshall's desk.

"Andrew, how are you?" I asked, my eyes scanning his desk for some kind of clue I could work with. All that was on his desk was a bunch of papers, nothing I could easily decipher.

"I'm good. It's nice to see you again, Jane. And your friend too." Dr. Marshall glanced over at Gabriel who stood against the door jam, his eyes taking in everything around us. Dr. Marshall then looked back at the detective. "I'm not sure how I can be of much more help. I told you everything that I know."

"Lie."

I spun around to find Lucifer standing next to Gabriel. Crap. Crap, crappy, crap, crap. Staring at Gabriel hard, I clenched my teeth and tried to mentally tell him not to move. Not to do anything that would give away that he was corporeal now.

Mandy placed a hand on my arm. "Did you see something?"

I stared at Gabriel for a few more seconds before my eyes fluttered closed and I lifted my hand to my head. "I'm feeling something all right. Something isn't right."

"Of course not." O'Connor scoffed. "We're wasting our time is what we are doing. We should be checking out her usual path home. Seeing what perverts might be living around where she travels. Not bothering this poor man."

"No, no." Dr. Marshall shook his head and took his glasses off and then back on. "You're not a bother at all. I just feel bad that I can't tell you where Clarissa is."

"That's a lie as well." Lucifer scoffed. "This guy knows more than he's telling now. I bet last time he didn't know where she was which was why I couldn't get a read on him, but now, he knows where this girl is. Don't you think, Gabe?"

Gabriel opened his mouth to answer, but I jumped in. "Dr. Marshall, you liked Clarissa, didn't you?"

Cocking his head to the side, so his hair fell over his face, Dr. Marshall gave me a small smile. "I like all my patients, of course."

"Lie."

I shot a look at Lucifer and then back to Dr. Marshall. "But you liked Clarissa more than the others?" I was reaching, but I couldn't think of another angle to go with.

"Well, yes." Dr. Marshall drew out. "She was a fine young woman. Very smart."

"And beautiful," I added, trailing my fingers along the top of his desk. "I've seen her pictures. She's a very pretty girl."

"Yes?" Dr. Marshall answered his brows furrowed. "It would be hard not to notice."

"And I bet you noticed her, didn't you?" I pried, tapping my nails on the surface of the desk. "With how often she came to see you, it would be only natural for you to be drawn to each other."

"Well, yes," Dr. Marshall stuttered, flustered by my questions. "She's a lovely woman. As I told her, anyone would be lucky to be with her."

"That's not a lie," Lucifer said.

"They were sleeping together," Gabriel said suddenly. I spun around panicking that he'd spoken while Lucifer was here. My eyes darted to Mandy and O'Connor watching in slow motion as they turned as one to Gabriel.

Lucifer's eyes brows crunched down as he tried to process what was going on. Even worse, Mandy asked, "How do you figure that?"

"They can see you?" Lucifer asked, his mouth gaping open. "And hear you?"

I waved Lucifer off, not able to answer him in front of everyone. Gabriel ignored him as well and answered Mandy, "It's pretty obvious. The way he lights up a bit every time he talks about her. Plus," - Gabriel pointed at a pink sweater on a chair in the corner - "I'm pretty sure that's a woman's sweater. Unless the good doctor here likes pink?"

Dr. Marshall jumped to his feet grabbing the sweater just as O'Connor started for it.

"Hand it over," O'Connor demanded, holding his hand out.

"It's my sister's." He held it close to him as if it were the most precious thing in the world. "She must have left it here."

"Still lying," Lucifer snapped at my side. "And we need to talk about this 'Gabriel being seen' thing. When were you going to tell me? Were you going to tell me at all?"

I pressed my lips into a thin line and gave him an incredulous look. Under my breath, I muttered, "Later."

During our exchange, O'Connor got the sweater from Dr. Marshall and held it out to Mandy to put in an evidence bag. "If it's your sister's, then the hair on this should match her DNA and not Clarissa's."

"Okay, fine." Dr. Marshall sighed. "It's Clarissa's. And he's right. We were sleeping together, but I didn't take her. I didn't kidnap her, I swear."

I glanced over at Lucifer. He glared at me but then grumbled, "He's telling the truth."

"He didn't do it," I told the detectives and then to Dr. Marshall. "Dr. Marshall knows where Clarissa is though, don't you? Jack was just a diversion to get us off the track."

O'Connor turned his fierce gaze back to the doctor who was quaking in his shoes now. "I didn't have anything to do with Jack's death, I swear. Clarissa doesn't want her parents to know where she is." He leaned in and lowered his voice. "They aren't nice people. You should hear some of the things Clarissa told me they did to her. Locking her up, denying her meals if she didn't go along with their rules." He shook his head sadly. "Really terrible."

"Then why didn't she go to the police?" Mandy asked, closing in on him with O'Connor. "If she was being abused, she should have said something. Hell, she's an adult. She could have left a long time ago."

"But they're paying her tuition," Dr. Marshall informed us. "They told her if she told anyone or tried to run away, they would cut her off. She'd lose everything. Her inheritance. Her degree. Everything."

"So, you helped her stage her supposed kidnapping," I offered, glancing at Gabriel for confirmation. He nodded.

"Yes," Dr. Marshall said solemnly. "We never wanted to get the police involved. We were surprised her parents even bothered to report it, let alone try to find her."

"What about her classes?" Mandy asked, brushing her hair away from her face. "You just said if she left, they'd take her money for school away. Why run away now and not after she graduated?"

Dr. Marshall sighed, taking his glasses off and rubbing his face. "I think it's better if you just talk to Clarissa yourself."

"Why can't you just tell us?" I was getting tired of all this game of twenty questions, especially, since Lucifer was staring daggers into my back. I had a feeling the moment we were alone, he'd be starting another round of questions.

Where the heck was Michael with my answers?

Dr. Marshall shook his head. "It's not something for me to share."

"This is a police investigation," O'Connor reminded him with a sneer. "You're already in a lot of trouble for that wild goose chase you sent us on. I suggest you tell us right now."

"O'Connor," Mandy placed her hand on his

arm. He glowered down at it, and she promptly removed it. "Let's just go find Clarissa, and then you can interrogate him back at the precinct until you're blue in the face."

The detective seemed to think about it for a moment. I almost thought he was going to argue with her, but then he nodded. "Come on, *Dr.* Marshall. Let's take a ride." O'Connor waved his hand forward, and Dr. Marshall started toward the door.

We all turned to follow, but O'Connor stopped in place. Turning back to me, he asked, "Where'd your assistant go?"

I looked where he pointed and saw Gabriel still standing there with Lucifer. Apparently, the effects of my blood had worn off during our conversation. The mention of Gabriel only made Lucifer scowl. Yep, I'd be getting my own interrogation once we got in the car.

"He's around," I said vaguely.

O'Connor frowned. "I don't want him disturbing the rest of the building. We don't want the precinct to get a bad reputation. It's bad enough we've got a psychic on the payroll."

I ignored his little jab and said, "I'll find him, don't worry. He's a free spirit, but he always finds his way back home." Mandy fought back a smile, and I winked at her. At least, someone thinks I'm funny.

O'Connor snorted but didn't argue. He led Dr. Marshall out of his office by the elbow. Once he was out of the room, Mandy came over to me.

"Where did Gabriel really go?" She searched the room as if she could find him.

"He's still here." I gestured with my head toward where Gabriel stood. "He's just incorporeal again."

Mandy's nose wrinkled. "Well, that's inconvenient. Maybe you shouldn't bring him in public if he's going to disappear? What would you have done if we had seen him disappear like with Michael?"

The lights in the room flickered, and I shot a look at Lucifer. His jaw clenched so tightly I worried he might break his teeth but more importantly, I feared he'd never talk to me again.

I shouldn't have kept it from him. Any of them. As soon as I knew what happened Michael and I should have told them. Or at least, not did it with anyone else until we knew for sure it was safe.

"What was that?" Mandy asked, her eyes going wide at the electrical malfunction.

I sighed and patted her on the shoulder. "I'll

handle it. Text me the address to wherever we're going, and I'll meet you there. I'm afraid I have some explaining to do."

Mandy frowned, worry etched on her face. I could tell she didn't want to leave me, but really, she couldn't help. This was my mistake, so I had to own up to it. No reason to get her in the middle of it.

"It's fine. I promise. I'll be right behind you," I assured her once more, nodding my head toward the door. "I'll lock up behind us."

"Oh-kay. If you're positive, you'll be safe." Mandy scanned the room and then crossed her arms over her chest. "Gabriel, wherever you are. You better take care of my girl. If you lay one finger on her head, I will personally make your existence a living hell."

I stifled a giggle and arched a brow at Gabriel, who only grinned. "Mandy," I laughed. "It's not Gabriel I'm worried about. It's the pissed off Devil whose feeling left out."

Mandy's brows rose. "Oh, you mean 'cause you've done it with Michael and Gabriel?"

The need to smack her upside the head was so strong, I had to clench my hands at my sides. Between clenched teeth, I said, "Yes, that's why. Now leave."

"Fine, fine. I know when I'm not wanted." She held her hands up in front of her and then pointed at me. "But no more hanky panky until this job is done. I'm scarred for life as it is."

"Out!" I jerked a finger at the door.

Mandy shot another look around the room before heading for the door. When she was gone, I hurried to shut it so I wouldn't have to worry about an audience. With the door shut and Mandy gone, I was finally alone with the angels.

Oh, joy.

Lucifer stalked across the room, pacing back and forth. I waited by Gabriel while he got his thoughts together. I knew I'd screwed up. I'd take my lickings, but I wasn't about to poke the bear.

"I'm disappointed in you," Lucifer said finally, his hands on his hips, his nostrils flaring wildly. "Of all of us, I have been trying to seduce you from the start and who gets to you first?" He gestured a hand at Gabriel.

"Actually, Michael did," Gabriel corrected him.

I glared at him. "Don't help." Then turning to Lucifer, I started toward him. "It was an accident. I cut my finger and Michael wanted to heal it. Then" - I held my hands out to the side swaying back and forth - "somehow, he ended up solid and ... you know."

"Of course," Lucifer scowled. "It's just like him to be the one to figure it out. He's always been the lucky one."

I had a feeling there was more to that statement than Lucifer was letting on, but I let it go. Everyone had family issues, why should angels be any different?

Stepping a bit closer to him, I smiled slightly, "If it makes you feel any better, he tried to walk through the table and ended up flipping over the couch."

A hint of a smile lifted the corners of Lucifer's lips. Encouraged by his smile, I added, "And Mandy walked in on us and saw the whole package, and he disappeared without his clothes, which, by the way, will not come with you." I pointed at the two of them as a warning. "I don't need a collection of angelically made clothing around my house. I have enough laundry of my own I don't do."

Lucifer chuckled. "I would have paid to see that. You should have snapped a picture. The great archangel with his feet over his head." He shook his head, smiling. "Priceless."

I waited until Lucifer stopped laughing and then asked, "So, are we good?"

Nodding, Lucifer said, "For now."

"Good, because we need to get going. Mandy's waiting for us to end this thing." I started toward the door with Gabriel and Lucifer on my tail.

After we got in the car and we drove down the street, Lucifer spoke up, "So, when do I get a turn?"

19

—————

The address Mandy sent me led us to a cute, pale blue house in one of those neighborhoods where soccer mom vans were the norm. Mandy and Detective O'Connor waited in front of the house with Dr. Marshall.

When I pulled up, Detective O'Connor started griping. "What took you so long? Do you think we run on your hours? Some of us would like to go home sometime today."

"Sorry to take away from your knitting needles, the spirits needed a bit of coddling," I smirked at Mandy who simply shook her head.

"I do not knit," Detective O'Connor growled.

Thankfully, the guys had taken off, saying they needed to confer with Michael, who had been MIA since he became corporeal. To be honest, I needed a bit of a break from them. All that testosterone was really getting to me. I just hoped I didn't need them to make any miraculous discoveries.

And poor Dr. Marshall looked like he was going to be sick. He probably just wanted to get this over with and get away from us crazy people.

Ironic since he worked with crazies for a living.

"Should we go inside?" I gestured toward the house. "Or did you want to wait outside all day? You're losing precious needling time."

O'Connor's face turned red. "I do not knit!"

Mandy and I ignored him and moved to the house. Dr. Marshall followed us, jumping in front to unlock the door. O'Connor brought up the rear, the steam still pouring out of his ears.

"Don't let her get to you," Mandy tried to calm him. "She only does it because you react so much."

"She's a child," O'Connor grumbled as we walked into the house. "She needs professional help."

"I can hear you," I twisted around to look at him. "And I've been in therapy before. They never really understood me."

"I can't imagine why," O'Connor snipped.

The inside of the house was as warm and

welcoming as the outside. It made me think of my grandmother's. Soft colors and a faint smell of chocolate chip cookies.

"Clarissa?" Dr. Marshall called out, searching around the room. "I'm home. Can you please come out here?"

We waited there for a few minutes, but no one came out. Detective O'Connor shifted in irritation and scowled at the doctor. "Where is she?"

Dr. Marshall's eyes went wide, and worry creased his forehead. "I don't know, she was here when I left this morning. I just told her I had to meet with you, but then I would be home." Without asking, Dr. Marshall moved through the house, calling Clarissa's name. O'Connor chased after him, probably trying to make sure he wouldn't take off on us.

"Where do you think she went?" Mandy asked me, searching around the living room for any sign of where she might have gone.

"I don't know, but she was definitely here." I pointed to the romance novel and the bag of cookies.

"That could be his, you don't know."

I lifted the pale pink bra off the floor with my

foot and quirked a brow. "And what about this? I don't think it's his size."

"Okay, so she was here, but that doesn't answer where she is now." Mandy waved a hand around the room. "I don't see a note."

Dr. Marshall and O'Connor came back into the room arguing. "She wouldn't have left without telling me. Not in her condition."

"Her condition?" Mandy asked.

The doctor shifted in place and frowned. "The reason Clarissa didn't want her parents to know is because she's pregnant. With my child."

Dun, dun, dun!

I knew it. I knew there was a reason for her to take off without telling her overbearing parents. They didn't want her to leave the house, they probably would have had a gasket if they found out she was pregnant and with her therapist's baby no less!

"Can you try and call her?" I asked. "Maybe she went to the store and forgot to tell you?"

"No, no. She wouldn't." Dr. Marshall's skin paled, and he kept rubbing his hands together. "She's been very careful about telling me where she goes in case she goes into labor."

Frowning, I couldn't figure out why he was so worried. Clarissa was pregnant, not disabled. *Please tell me he's not one of those kinds of guys*. I might have to punch him.

Our confusion must have been clear because Dr. Marshall explained, "Clarissa has a high-risk pregnancy. The likelihood of her going into premature labor is high. She can't get too distressed, or she could go early."

"Okay, okay," I held my hands up and came over to him. Rubbing his back, I made soothing noises. "It's okay, we'll find her." I nodded to Mandy who pulled out her walkie.

"Detective Stevenson here, we need a call into all the hospitals near Clarksville Street looking for a young woman, twenty-two, she's —" She paused and looked at Dr. Marshall. "How far along is she?"

"Almost twenty-five weeks." He gave a small smile, his eyes starting to water. "We were going to find out the sex of the baby this week."

"It's okay, I'm sure she's fine." I patted him on the back, while Mandy finished calling in the lookout for Clarissa.

"Is there anywhere else you think she might have gone?" O'Connor asked, shifting uncomfortably. Apparently, babies were not his thing or maybe it was the crying man in my arms.

Dr. Marshall shook his head. "She's been on bed rest. She wouldn't leave unless she had to."

Or forced to. A thought came to my mind.

"The parents," I suddenly said. "She's with her parents."

"What?" Mandy asked, putting her walkie up. "Why would you think that?"

"Well," I started and then pointed to the bag that was hidden beneath the coffee table. "She left her purse. Why would she do that? Even if she went to the hospital, most women would bring it with them."

Looking to Dr. Marshall, O'Connor asked, "Do her parents know where you live?"

Dr. Marshall shook his head. "Not that I know of. Not unless Clarissa contacted them, which she told me she wouldn't do until the baby was born."

"Maybe she had a change of heart?" Mandy offered up, and we all exchanged a look. If Clarissa had told her parents where she was, they wouldn't have been happy with her based on their previous treatment of her. Not for any reason. It was possible they had taken her home, even against her will.

"Let's go." O'Connor stomped toward the door a determined look on his face. "If she's a high risk as you say, then I have a feeling she's not going to be pregnant for very long."

We barreled out of the house and jumped into Mandy's car. I left my car at the doctor's house in favor of the police escort. We sped through the streets, the siren attached to the top of Mandy's car ringing our presence. People moved their vehicles out of our ways so quickly, it only took a few minutes to get back to the gated community.

"I need to get one of those." I gaped at the little red light attached to the top of the car. "It could really cut down on my commute time."

"I will arrest you if I see you with one." O'Connor snapped as we started up the Granes' yard. A crash from inside turned our speed walk into a sprint. We burst through the door and immediately heard the yelling.

"You can't keep me here," a voice I didn't recognize yelled from upstairs. "I'm a grown woman. I have rights."

"Clarissa, calm down. We are only trying to help you." Mrs. Granes said as we started up the stairs.

Dr. Marshall got there before we did, proving how much he cared for her. "Let her go!"

We crowded in around the landing. The sounds

were coming from Clarissa's bedroom. Rushing over to the door, I found the pretty blonde girl from the photo Mandy laying on her bed. You could clearly see her baby bump in the thin nightgown she wore, even as she fought against her parents as they tried to tie her down to her bed.

Dr. Marshall yelled her name again, and they glanced up from Clarissa.

Mr. Granes' face reddened, and he pointed a finger at the doctor. "You, you did this. Taking advantage of our poor daughter this way. How dare you show your face here!" He started toward the doctor, and O'Connor had the good sense to step in front of him. Mr. Granes tried to get around the detective but couldn't. Instead, he demanded, "Detective, arrest this man. He kidnapped our daughter and put that abomination in her."

O'Connor crossed his arms over his chest. "As far as I'm concerned, this man has done nothing wrong. It's you and your wife who have some explaining to do. Starting with why you are restraining a pregnant woman, who is clearly in distress."

Mandy and I rushed into the room once O'Connor had Mr. Granes out of the way. Mrs. Granes tried to stop us, an anxious look on her face.

"You can't take her. She needs to be here. With her father and me. We are the only ones who can take care of her."

I got in her face, making her back up a step. "She's a grown adult who can make her own choices. She might have some problems, but it seems to be that the biggest problem she has is you. Now, move before I make you move."

Mrs. Granes did the smart thing and moved out of the way. She hurried over to her husband who was still yelling at O'Connor. Mandy and I untied Clarissa and helped her up. Suddenly, Clarissa doubled over, crying out in pain. Water spewed from her and coated my shoes.

Forcing back a grimace, I shouted to Dr. Marshall, "Call the hospital now!"

"Oh my god, my baby," Clarissa gasped, grabbing her stomach.

"It's okay," I hushed, rubbing her back and exchanging a look with Mandy. "We're gonna get you some help."

Mandy helped me get her toward the bedroom door. O'Connor had put the dad in cuffs while the mother cried at his side. When Mrs. Granes tried to help us, I shrugged her off. "Haven't you done enough?"

After that, she dropped her hands, a look of shame covering her face. Good, she should be. I suddenly felt so thankful for my own mother. She might be quirky and a bit inappropriate at points, but she and dad would have never done anything like this to me.

We slowly made our way down the stairs with Dr. Marshall close at our backs. I grabbed a set of keys off the table on our way out the door. "Are these your car keys?" I asked Mrs. Granes. When she nodded, I continued, "Good, you can start making up for your actions by driving us to the hospital."

Mrs. Granes took the keys and rushed to her sedan. Opening the back door, she watched as we loaded Clarissa in the back. O'Connor took the still enraged father in the back of Mandy's vehicle. Mandy let Dr. Marshall replace her and got in the car with O'Connor. I slid into the front seat of Mrs. Granes' car, twisting around to keep an eye on Clarissa.

"Get going," I told Mrs. Granes. "And don't even think about going anywhere but the hospital."

Mrs. Granes started up the car, and we were on our way. We followed close behind Mandy and O'Connor as we sped toward the hospital. When we arrived, a nurse came out with a wheelchair and helped Dr. Marshall get Clarissa out of the car.

I watched from the waiting room as they took Clarissa to the maternity ward, Mandy at my side. We took a seat in the hard chairs that always filled places like this. For a hospital, you'd think they would want you to feel comfortable waiting, but the literal pain-in-the-butt chairs said otherwise. It implied more of an if-you're-not-dying-get-out kind of mentality. Like the dying didn't want a nice soft seat to sit their butt on while they waited for the All Mighty. I glanced over at Mandy. "Do you think she'll be okay?"

Mandy patted my shoulder. "I don't know. Babies aren't my specialty. Maybe you should ask your guys to put in a special request to the big guy."

I gave her a look. "I don't think it works that way."

"Can't hurt to try." She shrugged.

"Where'd O'Connor go?" I glanced around the waiting room but didn't see him or Mr. Granes in sight.

"He went ahead to the precinct to book Mr. Granes. Mrs. Granes will be following shortly after. We have officers coming to take her in now."

Mandy nodded toward where Mrs. Granes had disappeared with her daughter before.

"Can you even book them with anything?"

"Well, lying to the police for one and impeding the investigation," Mandy explained. "Holding their daughter against her will for another. I'm sure there are a few more things we can add on once Clarissa is fit to talk."

"You know what I don't get?" I asked. "She's only been missing for like a week. How did she hide her pregnancy from her parents this long?"

Mandy shrugged. "It's easier than you think. She's a thin girl, she probably didn't start showing until recently, and even that can be hidden by baggy clothes. How she kept calm in her condition though?" Mandy shook her head. "She must really want her baby."

"Yeah," I mused. Some people were meant to be parents. Clarissa's folks weren't among them. I just hoped she would learn from her parent's mistakes with her own child.

We waited downstairs for what seemed like forever when Dr. Marshall finally came back down. Mandy and I jumped to our feet. When he saw us, he diverted from the hospital door to walk towards us.

"How is she?" Mandy asked, a look of concern on her face.

"Did the baby live?" I blurted out, earning me a chastising look from Mandy. What? I wanted to know.

Dr. Marshall grinned, relief etched on his face. "She's fine. The baby's fine. While they had to put him in the NICU, the doctor says we shouldn't have anything to worry about."

"So, it's a boy?" I arched a brow.

Nodding, Dr. Marshall seemed like he might burst at the seams with joy at any moment. "Yes, we're calling him Michael."

I burst out laughing. Mandy hit me in the stomach with her elbow causing me to wince.

Dr. Marshall raised a curious brow.

"Ignore her," Mandy reassured him. "Ex-boyfriend issues."

"I see." Dr. Marshall adjusted his glasses. "Would you ladies like to see him? It was you who made this all possible after all."

Before Mandy could protest, I answered, "Of course!"

Mandy glared at me behind Dr. Marshall's back as he led us upstairs. See, Mandy had a thing about babies. She thought they were cute in theory, but she had a perpetual fear of holding them. Something about dropping them. Crazy, right? She handles guns every day and didn't drop those. I thought keeping a hold of a baby would be a hell of a lot easier.

We stopped in front of a window where they had several plastic-shielded basins. Inside were what I hoped were the babies.

Leaning over toward Mandy, I whispered, "Why do they look like a bunch of wrinkly old men?"

"Shh!" Mandy glanced toward Dr. Marshall, but he was too absorbed in looking at his baby boy to notice my comment.

Baby Michael didn't look much cuter than the rest of the babies, but I had to admit I still felt good to see the child safe and sound. Sure, I might have started out this little consulting job simply for money, but to know that I, well, the guys and I, had done some real good here …

Mandy interrupted my goody-goody feelings by telling Dr. Marshall, "He's adorable. Thank you for sharing him with us."

Nodding distractedly, he didn't notice much when we snuck away. Out of view of the babies and their adoring parents, we sagged. Chuckling, I turned to Mandy. "Is it just me or were some of those babies verging on gorilla territory?"

Mandy laughed and shoved me. "That's not nice. They're cute."

"To their parents maybe." I sniffed. "My kid won't be like that. She'll have a perfectly rounded bald head and her poop will come out in perfect little cupcake-sized packages."

"You're delusional." Mandy rolled her eyes as we entered the waiting room once more.

"So, what now?" I turned away from Mandy and back toward the hospital exit.

"What do you mean?" Mandy raised an eyebrow at me.

"We found Clarissa, saved the day, and arrested the bad guy. I get paid now, right?" I rubbed my thumb and fingers together. "Mama needs some scratch."

Mandy laughed. "Yeah, you'll get paid, but probably not for a few days." She lowered her voice, but even that wasn't enough to mask the glee in her eyes. "I also think you need to fill out some more paperwork." She let the words hang in the air while I tried to decide how much I liked money just then, especially when I wouldn't even be getting paid today. "I'm going to get a ride back with one of the officers. You're free to come along," she added unhelpfully.

I grimaced. I'd had about enough excitement for one day. I just wanted to spend the rest of my day off in my own house. Preferably with a bottle of wine and binge watching my favorite show. Doing paperwork definitely wasn't in that equation.

"Can you just drop me off at Dr. Marshall's?"

"You don't want to do paperwork?" Mandy practically exploded with laughter.

"That's a hard pass." I shook my head. "Helping out has been fun, but I need a little me time."

Mandy gave me a sly grin. "Don't you mean you need a little angel time?"

My face heated, and I shoved her shoulder. "No, I don't."

"Fine, I'll let you have your day off." She glanced up at the darkening sky. "Or what's left of it."

I sighed. "If there's another emergency, just leave me out of it. At least for today." A worn-out feeling sunk into my bones. "Or make that for the rest of the year."

"It wasn't that bad." Mandy smiled at me.

"I don't know. I tempted to leave the crime

solving to the professionals. Right now, I'd rather be serving alcohol to the drunkards of Blessed Falls than listening to irate parents."

Mandy laughed. "Just wait until you have a kid of your own."

"Oh god no," I groaned. "That's not going to happen for a very long time." If ever. The guys were immortal, I didn't see how I would ever want to give them up for a normal life. After all, who was going to be able to compare once you've had mind-blowing orgasms with a real-life archangel?

20

Three days later, I signed the final form in front of me and handed it back to the policewoman behind the desk. The policewoman handed me an envelope that would have my very first paycheck as a consultant in it.

"Thank you very much." I grinned at her.

She waved me off and turned back to her computer.

Greedily, I ripped open the envelope and held my paycheck in my hand. The numbers on it made my eyes widen. This was more than I made at the bar in a week by far. Even with tips!

"That didn't take you long." I turned toward the sound of Mandy's voice and smiled.

"Had to see if it was worth it." I shrugged. I'd taken three days before I finally showed up at the precinct to collect my check. If I was honest, I needed a little space. I liked helping people, but combine that with horny angels, and it would wear on any person.

"And was it?" Mandy nodded toward my check.

Folding the paper over, I tucked it in my back pocket. "Maybe."

"Maybe?" Mandy cocked her head to the side. "So, you wouldn't do it again?"

I shook my head. "I wouldn't say that."

"Good, because we have another case." Mandy gestured toward the back with her head. "You in?"

I pretended to think about it for a minute, tapping my chin and everything and then said, "Sure, I guess I could help out."

Mandy laughed. "So nice of you to fit us into your busy schedule."

I shrugged and followed Mandy to the back. "What can I say, I'm a giver."

I spent the next few hours getting debriefed on the next case. A diamond had been stolen from a vault. I was pretty sure it was an inside job. I didn't need the angels to tell me that. It was too neat, but it was sure damned funny when Gabriel clued me into where the diamond was stashed. Take that pasty-faced manager.

"What do you have planned now?" Mandy asked me afterward.

Grinning like a fiend, I jerked my head toward the exit. "Come on, I've got something to show you."

Mandy followed me to my car, a curious look in her eyes.

"Where are we going?" she asked but I shook my head not answering her.

We drove down the street and toward the place I had in mind. I parked the car in front of the shop with a large window in the front. I'd found it online. It had office space and even a bathroom and kitchenette.

One call to my dad and it had been mine. I tried not to bother my parents for money often. I wanted to be my own person, get by on my own. But this place? I couldn't let it go because of a lack of collateral or credit.

I brought Mandy to the front of the shop and swept an arm toward the window, a proud smile on my lips.

"*Gotcha?*" Mandy arched a brow as she took in the green and white letters on the window. "Why didn't you just say, 'I'm pretending to be a psychic but really, I see angels, so let me help you out?'"

I sighed and waved her off. "First, that name is way too big. These letters are like ten bucks a pop. Besides, what better way to get people to trust you than to tell them you're lying?"

"You are a crazy person." Mandy shook her head. "What are you going to do? Tell fortunes?"

"No," I scoffed. "I'm going to be a private detective."

Mandy's brow furrowed her hands on her hips. "Don't you need a license for that?"

"Nope," I said with a pop of my lips. "Psychics are excluded from that little rule."

"But don't you think people will figure out that you're a fake?" Mandy said incredulously.

"Nah, people believe what they want to believe." I headed into the office, showing my new place off. "Plus, I've already got a few calls from people wanting my help."

"Really?" Mandy asked, taking in the desk and chair set up I had already put in. "So, how are you going to do this, the bar, and help with the cops?"

"I'll figure it out, and if it comes down to it, I'll just quit the bar," I smirked. Bill was just gonna love that.

Mandy wandered around the office, opening and closing doors. Nodding her head, she seemed to approve. "You'll need a coffee maker and business cards."

"Already ordered." I plopped down into my chair and swiveled around.

Sighing, Mandy sat on the edge of my desk. "Well, it seems like you've thought of everything."

"I still need a secretary." I wagged my eyebrows at her.

"Uh, no." Mandy held a finger up. "I'm happy where I am, thank you very much. Besides, you can just make your guys take turns. They can turn corporeal, now, can't they?"

"Pfft." I rolled my eyes. "I'm not opening a vein every time I need something filed. Also, when they go solid, they aren't really thinking with their heads."

"Ugh." Mandy made a face. "Just promise me you won't do it in the office."

I held my hands up. "Can't promise that."

"Fine, then I'm not coming to visit you." She

stood from the desk and headed for the door. I jumped up from my seat to head her off.

"Hey now, don't be like that. I'm sure we can work something out. I'll buy one of those things of disinfectant wipes and keep it by the desk. You know one of those with the little holes in the top?" I gestured like I was pulling one of them out of their container.

Mandy shook her head. "Nope, I'm not doing it. I'll just see you at the precinct."

"Oh, come on, now. You can't expect me to go down there all the time. I've got a business to run." I put my hands on my hips and blocked the doorway.

Mandy smiled. "That you do." Patting me on the shoulder, she pushed me aside to leave.

My cheeks starting to ache from smiling, I turned back to my office. I couldn't believe it was really mine. I'd taken the first step into real adulthood, and I couldn't be happier.

"What are you so happy about?" Gabriel asked, appearing in my chair.

"Yes, you do seem particularly proud of yourself." Michael came out from the bathroom, his eyes scanning the area.

"This is my new shop." I held my hands up waving them around. "What do you think?"

"I think it could use a bed back here," Lucifer drawled, exiting my small kitchen area.

"I'm not going to sleep here." I scowled at him.

Lucifer grinned wolfishly. "I wasn't talking about for sleeping."

I pointed a finger at him. "I'm not doing that here either. It's my place of business, not a hookup pad."

"Why can't it be both?" Gabriel asked, and I smirked at him.

"Because I don't need potential clients walking in on us. Besides, what will people think when they see me with different guys all the time?" I sat on the edge of the desk.

Michael lifted an elegant shoulder. "Tell them the truth."

I laughed. "Oh, yeah. 'Cause that will go over well. Oh, these are just my boyfriends, that only become solid when they want a little Jane action."

"Boyfriends?" Lucifer arched a brow and grinned, leaning on the desk next to me. "We're your boyfriends now?"

I blushed. "Well, uh, I didn't mean it like that."

I stared down at the desk as they started to close in on me.

"Does that mean we get privileges?" Michael asked, and I glanced at him.

"What kind of privileges are we talking about?" I said suspiciously.

"Like, we get to have an opinion on your life," Gabriel interjected.

I snorted. "And you don't do that now?"

"Yeah." Gabriel grinned. "But now it actually means something."

Lucifer put his hand up. "I was talking about something more substantial. Like getting to participate in shower time." He leered at me, making me squirm in place.

"I'll think about it," I conceded

"I'd like to weigh in on this as well." Michael pressed against my back, buzzing tingles shooting down my spine. "Especially, those times you complain about needing new batteries, so you can relax."

And my panties were destroyed.

"I think you might need a bit of relaxing time now, don't you?" Lucifer exchanged a look with the guys.

"She definitely seems tense." Gabriel stood from his chair and leaned over the desk.

Chuckling nervously, I tucked a loose hair behind my ear. "I'm fine, really, guys. No stress here. As cool as a cucumber." When they didn't stop looking at me like they wanted to devour me, I cleared my throat and said, "Hey, Lucifer. Have you ever heard of fire sauce?"

THANK YOU FOR READING!

**Curious about what happens to Jane,
Michael, Lucifer, and Gabriel next?**

Find out in Heaven's a Beach!

AUTHOR'S NOTE

Dear reader, if you REALLY want to read the next Her Angels novel- I've got a bit of bad news for you.

Unfortunately, **Amazon will not tell you when the next comes out.**

You'll probably never know about my next books, and you'll be left wondering what happened to Jane and the gang. That's rather terrible.

There is good news though! There are three ways you can find out when the next book is published:

1) You join our mailing list by clicking here.

2) You can also follow Erin on her Facebook Page. We always announce new books in those places as well as interact with fans.

3) You follow us on Amazon. You can do this by going to the store page (or clicking this link) and clicking on the Follow button that is under the author picture on the left side.

If you follow me, Amazon will send you an email when I publish a book. You'll just have to make sure you check the emails they send.

Doing any of these, or all three for best results, will ensure you find out about my next book when it is published.

If you don't, Amazon will never tell you about my next release. Please take a few seconds to do one of these so that you'll be able to join Jane and the gang on their next adventure.